Murderous Interruptions

The Veils of Parallel Times Trilogy
— Book 2 —

C.J. Carson

Published by:
Rustic Barn Door Publishing
www.cjcarsonauthor.com
cjcarsonauthor@gmail.com

ISBN: 978-1-954356-01-6

Editing and Interior Design by Jessica Tilles/TWA Solutions

For my mother, who, for as long as I can remember, was my cheerleader and always inspired me to follow my dreams, providing her unconditional love and guidance for my entire family and me.

Acknowledgments

My eternal gratitude to my life partner, who has supported all my artful endeavors in this lifetime.

Gratitude to my amazing daughter, Virginia, who continues to join me on this journey, tirelessly reviewing and providing feedback for The Veils of Parallel Times as it unfolds.

A special thanks to my editor, Jessica Tilles, for her dedication and diligent work, helping me bring yet another book successfully to my audience.

Heartfelt thanks to M.L. Hamilton for her wonderful book cover designs, capturing the true essence of The Veils of Parallel Times.

With a humble heart, I thank all my friends and family who have supported me unconditionally and encouraged my life's journey.

Many thanks to The Carolina Forest Author's Club members, who have encouraged and inspired me to move forward with completing this second book in the trilogy of The Veils of Parallel Times.

Prologue

Over the past year, my life has been a whirlwind, filled with significant trauma, excitement, joy, intrigue, and deep sorrow, starting about six months ago.

My driven, all too predictable, mundane life was ripped apart at the seams!

Working at my office late one evening, a total stranger brutally attacked me. I would learn later his name was Makya. That dreadful event brought me back to a crucial fork in the road of my life. I could have continued down the same path that brought me to this point or changed direction. It was then that I realized the universe would have thrown obstacles in my way until I chose the road that would lead me to my true destiny.

In my natural life, I had been growing increasingly aware of how the elements influenced people, both physically and energetically. Even scientifically, this seemed like an objective, measurable, and logical conclusion, since people consisted primarily of matter and water. I would like to say I figured this out all on my own, but my great-grandmother imparted this wisdom to me.

Time was an entirely different subject, with which I had yet to come to terms. I had always believed in the time line for the life of mankind—birth, living life, and death. I had always believed that, literally. Well, recent events in my life made me aware that those rules might not apply to me.

The last year was not entirely bad. It had opened up to me in so many miraculous ways. I had made some fantastic new friends and helped others in ways I never could have dreamed possible. I moved into a fabulous new apartment complex called the Summit. After a long and trying period in my life, things felt like they were turning around. Then, on New Year's Eve, I was happy to end that year and start anew when I became engaged. The tragic disappearance of my fiancé, Josh, the love of my life, quickly cut the bliss of that moment short. Gone without a trace, leaving only a blood-stained apartment behind and no clue as to Josh's fate. My mere existence became tumultuous, and I never imagined it could have unraveled so quickly again. For a few months, I went into seclusion. Finally, one day in March, George Pappas, an old friend of my grandfather's, suggested I might spend a long weekend at his summer home, a beautiful farm in Acton, Maine. So, I guess this story would begin there. Let me take you back to that part of my life when I stood on the edge of understanding the influence nature's elements and time had over events in my life and those around me.

Chapter 1

It was Friday morning, in mid-March, and for the first time in months, I was looking forward to the weekend. The night before, I had packed a small bag, and about ten o'clock, I headed out to George Pappas' beautiful farm in Acton, Maine, which never disappointed, for a much-needed weekend. A short ride into the country from Stanford, on the way, I stopped at a local farm for fresh vegetables and local honey. Arriving, I pulled into the driveway of his big yellow farmhouse, which was always blessed with the greenest pastures, the most amazing daffodils, and a colorful parade of tulips. When I stepped out of the car, a soft breeze greeted me, carrying the smell of the lilacs that were in full bloom all over the property.

That weekend turned out to be the best medicine I could have ever imagined. I relaxed in the yard during the days and had a fire in the evenings. My visit seemed to go by too quickly, so Monday morning I stayed for the day and left later that afternoon. After all, why not get an extended weekend in? I didn't want to leave, anyway! So that was it. I spent the afternoon sitting under my favorite apple tree to catch up on some reading.

The warmth of the sun and the slight breeze in the air lulled me to sleep. Just before dusk, the wind picked up, and the clouds rolled in, waking me from my nap. I opened my eyes and peered up from my chair to find a young girl over me. The same girl that had been appearing to me over the past several months. She pointed toward the field behind a gate that had swung open, and for the first time, she spoke aloud. "It's time."

"Time? Time for what? Can you please tell me, once and for all, who you are and what you want from me? I don't understand any of this."

With a gentle and calming smile, she folded her hands in front of her. "You know me. You don't remember me, but trust me, you know me."

"I'm sorry, but I think somehow you have mistaken me for someone else."

Reaching out, she placed her hand in front of my eyes. "I am here to help you. You don't recognize me because the circumstances of your life have covered your eyes to the truth. I am you in your youth. I have traveled here to help you remember your gifts. You need to be reminded because of the vital role they play in the life you are living now.

"I am here to tell you it is time for you to rise up, fully embrace your gifts, and get past this dark place in your life.

Then and only then can you come out into the light again and walk your path. Do you want to stay stuck in this version of your existence? Nothing good can come of that. Not for you, not for your friends, and certainly not for Josh, the love of your life!"

I couldn't speak, but as the young girl pulled her hand away from my eyes, she pointed to the field again. A tall, powerful white horse galloped out of the woods, across the field, and through the open gate.

"This is your mount, and he has been with you in many lifetimes. He takes you where you need to go safely, and shields you from impending dangers. Whenever he comes to you, it's your cue that you are about to go on a significant journey. Please, let him carry you today as this is a door-opening opportunity, one you have missed in the past."

With that, she offered a lift to his back. As I climbed up, I looked back. "I still don't understand?"

"I promise, you will. The knowledge will come. You have an ancestor to visit."

I turned toward the gate to see a thick layer of fog had formed.

Placing her hand on my leg, she added, "This is a thin veil you must travel through. I have brought you here to help you understand your gift for moving between dimensions. A gift you haven't remembered since you were very small."

Reaching up, she gave the horse a tap on his haunches, and we trotted off across the field, through that veil of fog, and into the forest. I wasn't traveling long when darkness settled over the woods, and the air became chilled and damp. I was getting nervous that I might not find my way back out of the woods in the dark. I stopped at a brook to give my horse a quick break and a cool drink. As I raked my fingers through his mane, something caught his attention. Nodding his head, he whinnied. When I looked up, I spotted a campfire in the distance. As I walked him in that direction, I found a heavyset elderly woman with long dark braids sitting at, and stoking the fire. Moving in for a closer look, she wore a dress made of brown suede and was wrapped in an animal skin blanket, shielding her from the cold.

I didn't recognize her, but somehow, she was oddly familiar to me. Without speaking a word, she reached out, beckoning me. I could feel a connection that drew me in as I slid down from my horse and joined her. She opened the blanket and, as I sat down, she held me in her arms to warm me by the fire. I was suddenly in my youth again, swept up in warmth and safety I hadn't felt for a very long time.

Raising her arm, the woman drew my attention to the flames, and as I stared into the blazing fire, I couldn't pull my eyes away. It was as if it was speaking to me, its warmth drawing me in.

"This is your truth, my daughter of my daughter's son. You are at your best and can do your work in this lifetime when you accept that you are one with the earth, fire, water, and elements. Only when you embrace them, can you move toward your true destiny. You are a rare spirit in that you are blessed with many gifts that you are yet to discover and recognize. Yours is not an easy path unless you embrace it. I am always here; you have only to think of me, and I will be in your thoughts to help you, as are all your ancestors.

"Little Bird, you have traveled and lived in many times and dimensions. Think of time as a path that runs horizontally, but many paths are layered, one on top of the other, in a horizontal pattern.

"You have the ability to move through them, not only in time, but from one dimension to another. It was the element of water in the stream that brought you to me. Keep your routes planted firmly into the earth, for that will ground you and keep you balanced. Tonight, I want you to look into the dancing flames and listen to them speak to you. It is past the time for you to begin to understand your truth, my dear. You do not have the luxury of putting it off any longer."

Gazing into the flames, I saw visions of a young woman riding my white horse. As the horse moved up a hill and into a green meadow, the young girl was now a young woman. As I studied her, she looked nothing like me, but I felt like I was watching my memory unfold. She was riding on a horse with a knight that looked like he was from medieval times. As the horse reached the top of the meadow, I knew the woman in the vision was an image of me, and when the valiant knight turned to me, a chill coursed through my entire body. Although his face was unfamiliar, his deep blue eyes caught me off guard. Those eyes, those beautiful eyes. I would know them anywhere.

When I turned from the fire to respond, the woman hushed me. "You have much work to do, my dear, now rest." She held me in her arms, swallowing me up in the most comforting sleep I could remember for a very long time, maybe ever.

Hours later, the warm glare of the sun's first light sliced through the trees of the forest, waking me from a sound sleep. The air was cool and crisp, and I was laying next to the fire that had burned down to smoldering coals. Suddenly, realizing I wasn't dreaming, I was in unfamiliar surroundings. I remembered the woman I had met the evening before, but she was not within eyeshot. Glancing around to get my bearings, it was shocking to be sitting in the middle of a small clearing of the woods. Several teepees made of tall tree branches wrapped in animal skins sat along the edge of the clearing. Standing and sliding out from under the animal skin blanket, I looked down to see myself dressed in unfamiliar clothes, and leather moccasins covering my feet. I had the strange sensation I was in a familiar place, but still not where I belonged.

Before I took one step, I scanned the area. Then something compelled me to approach one of the dwellings. As I drew closer, an Indian brave stepped out. Grabbing me by the arm, he pulled me into the teepee and shoved me to the ground. Walking to the edge of the space, he retrieved a large round basket and shot it at me with such force I thought it might fray. Shocked, I gazed up at him, he looked oddly familiar, but it was his eyes that gave him away. These new experiences were teaching me that the eyes were indeed the window to the soul. Those dark brown eyes were those of a man I knew all too well. Makya! Could this be Makya? Had I known him through other lifetimes? Although he spoke in a different tongue, it somehow translated perfectly for me.

He was angry and started barking. "You are a lazy dreamer. Why you insist on leaving our dwelling and choose to lay with the fire in place of me is a mystery. You need to do your gathering, and you are late in starting your day. I am off to hunt. You will obey me and begin behaving like a squaw worthy of me."

I heard footsteps outside as someone was approaching. "Calian, are you coming? We are late; the morning is half over."

Stunned, my eyes widened. *Makya?* Although the man called him Calian, the spirit was too familiar. It was the evil spirit I'd come to know as Makya! It didn't look like him, but it was his temperament.

As I pushed up to my knees, Calian glared down at me, striking out in my direction. Although his hand never touched me, a force knocked me back to the ground. As I raised my hand to him, he grabbed my wrist, twisting it, and forced me back to the ground.

"You know better. Do not use your powers on me. I will strike you down every time. You are no match for me!"

Panic rose in me as I struggled to understand what was happening. If this brave was indeed Makya by a different name, how did we get here?

Pushing through the opening in the structure, he paused without turning to me. "Do not return this afternoon unless you have filled that basket with berries and some healing herbs. You must learn your place and mind your responsibilities. Do not make me the laughingstock of this tribe one more time!"

I listened to his footsteps as he jogged off, mounted his horse, and rode away before I got up from the ground.

Knowing I had to escape and find my way back to George's, and my own time, I didn't want to attract any unwanted attention, so I picked up the basket and went out in search of my horse. As I walked by the doused firepit, I picked up the animal skin blanket I had slept under the night before. Trying to be inconspicuous, I moved subtly and found my horse at the edge of the clearing. Looking up toward the trail I had ridden in on the night before, I untied him and moved in that direction.

A woman's voice pleaded behind me. "Where are you going, Winona? A squaw is not permitted to ride off on her own into the woods."

As I tossed the animal skin over the horse's neck and leaped to his back, she approached and stood right in front of him, blocking my way. She lifted the basket from the ground. "I believe you forgot something. You know this is forbidden. Calian will be very angry again."

Looking down from the horse, I peered into her eyes. "Claudia?"

She swiftly recoiled. "What is a Claudia?"

Quickly coming back to my senses, ignoring the question, I assured her, "I am only going just beyond the forest to a clearing. I won't be far. I will be back before nightfall. I promise I'll be fine."

Turning my horse and entering the woods, I headed back up the trail in the direction I had come from when I found the woman at the fire. I knew I had to at least put some distance between me and the tribe before they realized I was not returning. Remembering my horse had followed the river through the woods, I waded into the water, moving upstream to cover my tracks.

I contemplated finding a place to settle in for some sleep as the damp, cool air of nightfall was blanketing the forest. Suddenly, I saw a clearing ahead and an open tree line. Maybe it was George's farm!

Picking up the pace, I trotted up to the clearing. Although it felt familiar, the landscape had somehow changed. Moving further into the clearing, I gazed down to the other side of the meadow, only to see more trees and forest. The land that stretched out in front of me was definitely not George's farm. I stopped for the night. Climbing down from my horse, I tied him to a tree in the field where he could graze on the grass. I used my basket to forage for something to eat and was fortunate to find some wild blueberries and acorns. I gathered wood to keep a small fire burning through the night. As it grew dark, I brought my horse down out of the field to the trees to provide us some cover from the elements and any intruders.

When I awoke hours later, I felt extremely unsettled. There was a chill in the air, and it appeared to be dusk and getting dark all over again. Stopping, I hesitated to collect my thoughts. I looked up to see that I was, once again, on George's farm.

Wait, was this real? What seemed real was a blur. Did I just fall asleep and dream of my experience with that young girl and the older woman at the fire? Of course, that was it; I was dreaming. That was the only thing that made sense. Although it all was shocking, I knew I needed to pull myself together and head home. I found myself a bit disappointed; I had slept a good part of my last day at the farm, but I must have still needed the rest.

Getting up, I reached for my book, but much to my dismay, I couldn't find it. That was odd. What could have happened to it? I moved around the tree, searching the ground for it, to no avail.

Before it got any darker, I walked down from the pasture toward the farmhouse. As I approached the long driveway, my car was not there, and things went from odd to bizarre right away. I reached into my pocket for the key to the house, but it was empty. Shit, it must have fallen out of my pocket into the grass. The sensor light at the end of the barn went on, lighting the driveway, reminding me that George always hid a key in the rock wall near the mailbox. I quickly retrieved it and let myself into the house.

Once I got through the back door and had a minute to think, I had a sinking feeling that my stalker and attacker, Makya, could be back. Maybe he took my car to keep me stranded here for the night. I moved through the kitchen to retrieve my bag and cell phone from the counter. They were missing as well. *Are you kidding me?* I moved over to use the landline, and much to my relief, it was working. I called my friend, Claudia, but she didn't answer. Then, I tried my mother, again no answer. I made one last attempt to reach someone and called the Summit.

"Hello. Thank you for calling the Summit. This is Sandy Turner. How can I help you?"

"Hello, Sandy, this is Allie. Is Guile there, please?"

"Hi, Allie, it's great to hear your voice. No, Guile has left for the evening. Can I take a message?"

"No, that's okay."

Hanging up, I knew I had to remain calm and think. It was seven o'clock. Stuck with no car, no cell phone, and no wallet, I called a cab to take me to my apartment at the Summit. I would get some money to pay the driver when I got there. My friend, Claudia, or Dakota, my landlord, should be there soon.

Chapter 2

The cab was there within ten minutes, and we were on our way. As we arrived at the Summit, I tapped the driver on the shoulder. "Could you please give me a minute? I will be right back with your fare."

"Sure, no problem."

As I turned to get out of the car, Henry, the evening parking attendant, opened the door and looked quite shocked. "Ms. Callahan?"

"Yes, Henry. I need to go upstairs and get this young man his fare. I seem to have lost my bag and have no cash or credit card on me."

Reaching into his pocket, he stepped over to the driver's window. "I've got this, Ms. Callahan."

"Oh, thank you, Henry. That's very kind."

As the cab drove away, Henry turned to me. "I am so glad to see you, Ms. Callahan. Where have you been?"

"Why thank you, Henry. I was staying at a friend's home in the country. Do you know if Claudia, Jake, or Dakota are here? I really need to speak with them."

"I am sure they will want to talk to you as well. They're all at the York Harbor Inn this evening. Let me get the car and give you a ride there. They'll be so happy to see you."

He brought the car around and opened the door for me.

"Thank you for the ride, Henry. I think someone has stolen my car, and I couldn't get to the Inn without your help."

"You're entirely welcome, Ms. Callahan."

When we arrived, he got out of the car to open my door. "I am sure everyone will be so happy to see you. What a wonderful surprise. You can find them in one of the dining halls."

Feeling a little confused, I faintly smiled. "Why, thank you, Henry."

As I stepped into the lobby of the York Harbor Inn, the maître d greeted me at the door. "How can I help you, Miss? Is someone joining you or will you be dining alone this evening?"

"I am looking for Claudia Buchanan? I was told she was here."

"Yes, but of course. Claudia is one of our guests of honor this evening. Please follow me."

He led me to one of a few banquet halls and opened the door. When I stepped in, the room went silent, and I had everyone's attention. As I glanced around, everyone I knew was there. I thought for a minute I had walked into a surprise party for me, but the surprise was on me.

My mother rushed into my arms and started sobbing. "Allie, you're here." Turning to everyone in the room, she beamed. "Oh, my God, she's here!"

I looked over her shoulder to see Claudia rushing to my side. "Where have you been? We have all been so worried!"

"What are you talking about? You know I went to George's for the weekend. For crying out loud, I told you I was going."

Claudia grabbed my mother and me by the arms and dragged us out and down the hall to the ladies' room. "What on God's green earth are you saying?" She paused for a minute, took a few steps away from me, and then turned. "Wait a minute! Just wait one minute! This does not make any sense."

"I don't get it. What doesn't make sense? Look, Claudia, you knew George offered me the farmhouse, and that I was going there for the weekend. You even called me on my cell phone Friday night while I was up there."

My mother took my hands in hers and backed me up to a seat in the powder room. Sitting down beside me, she looked over at Claudia. "I think we need to slow down and talk Allie through this." Cradling my face, she turned it toward hers. "Honey, you went to George's for the weekend, but that was six months ago."

"What? No, you're mistaken. It was four days ago."

There was a knock on the door. It was Jake. "Hello in there. Is everyone okay?"

Claudia got up and went to the door, pulling it open. "It's just us in here. You can come in."

Walking over to me, he kneeled. "We're all so glad to see you, Allie. We have been worried sick."

I couldn't hold it in any longer, and the tears started falling, drenching my face, as I started rambling. "I don't understand any of this, Jake. I went to George's for the weekend to unwind and relax. The time had gone by so quickly, so today I decided to stay the entire day to relax and enjoy the sunshine. I packed the car early in the afternoon, and went to my favorite reading place up near the pasture, and got comfortable. I fell asleep, and when I woke up, it was getting dark. When I headed down to the farmhouse, my car was gone. Once I was in the house, my bag was missing. My concern level was escalating, and I wanted to get out of there as quickly as possible. I was worried that my things missing might be the work of Makya again. I called a cab for a ride to the Summit, and from there, Henry gave me a ride here to find you, Claudia, and Dakota. What am I missing?"

Claudia kneeled next to Jake. "I don't want to scare you, Allie, but you're missing about six months."

My mother reached out to me and took my hand. "Honey, you did go to George's farmhouse, but that was six months ago. When you didn't come back to town that Monday, Claudia and I drove up to find you. Your car was there and packed to come home, your bag was on the counter in the kitchen, and we even found your book up under the apple tree where you say you were sitting and fell asleep. Payne, Jake, and everyone have been looking for you for months. You just disappeared without a trace."

My head was spinning, and there was a second knock on the door. It was Dakota. "Hello in there. Are we moving this party down here?"

Jake got up and opened the door. "I don't think so. I was just going to suggest that we come back to the banquet hall and finish our meal."

In all the excitement of the moment, I completely missed the fact that something important was happening there tonight, and I didn't even know what it was.

"Claudia, just exactly what is that dinner for this evening?"

Jake moved toward the door. "Maybe we should give these two a minute before they come back to the reception."

As the three of them left the room, I reached out to Claudia. "What the heck is happening to me? I just don't get it. None of this makes any sense, but then that is the way my life has been going for the past several months. I don't know why I'm surprised."

Suddenly, realizing I was rambling, I stood. "Claudia, what reception is Jake talking about? You haven't gone and got married or anything as important as that without me, have you?"

"No, not quite."

"What does that mean? Not quite! Did I miss one of the most important days of your life?"

She took my hands in hers. "This is our rehearsal dinner. We are getting hitched tomorrow, and you, my friend, have made it back just in time to be my maid of honor!"

Pulling her into my arms, I embraced her. "Oh, my God, Claudia, I would be honored." Then I pushed her back. "But only under one condition!"

"Oh yeah, and what would that be?"

"That you never say the word hitched again! This is really way too important of an event to call it anything less than getting married or taking your vows!"

Claudia pressed her index finger to her lips. "Hmm, well, you sure do drive a hard bargain, my friend, but that's a deal! Hey, we have a lot of catching up to do tonight, so what do you say we go back to the dinner, get it over with, and go to our room and get ready for tomorrow?"

As we entered the reception, everyone stood in applause. Leaning into Claudia, taking her hand, we moved through the room. "Look at me, stealing the show from you tonight, on one of the most important events of your life. It's just not right!"

"Are you kidding? I am happy to share the limelight with you. In fact, this is the greatest wedding gift you could have ever given me. I was dreading tomorrow without my lifetime friend by my side."

"You mean your bestie by your side!"

"Yes, for sure, and the day will be just perfect now."

As we moved to the front of the dining room, Claudia's father, Ben Buchanan, was standing with the microphone in his hand. "Well, here is my princess now. You are just in time for a toast, my dear." He turned to me. "First, I would like to say how grateful we are that Allie, Claudia's best friend, who has been like a second daughter to me, has made it safely back to us." He stepped closer to his daughter. "Claudia will always be my little princess. I'm sure she isn't happy that I still call her that to this day." Turning to her, he took another step forward. "Honey, I couldn't be prouder of you than I am tonight. You have grown into a beautiful young woman, and it is not lost on me that your beauty on the inside far surpasses what we all see here before us tonight.

"The world is at your feet, my dear. You have grown into the most wonderful woman and an incredible artist. It certainly shows in every piece of work you do. While your paintings are executed with a brush, the real magic you capture on canvas emanates from your heart. You have acquired your mother's and grandmother's ability to see and paint the world in the most remarkable ways. Your mother once told me that you could capture the goodness and beauty in everything you saw around you. I am sure she is with us tonight, on this most important occasion."

As tears streamed from his eyes, he lifted a box off of the table behind him. "I hope you don't mind, but I took the liberty of having something made for you. Here, honey, this is from your mother and me." He handed it to her. "I hope you like it. I think it is fit for a princess."

Turning to me, Claudia put the box in my hands, lifted the lid, and handed it to her father. As she unwrapped the white tissue, unfolding it to reveal the contents, she cried.

Reaching in, she lifted a simple gold crown with painted white flowers woven through the base. At the top were three points, with a diamond in the center enhanced by a deep teal sapphire on either side.

At first, she couldn't speak, as everyone in the room reacted at the same time. Finally, her voice cracked. "Is this—"

"I had this made with the gems from your mother's engagement ring."

Throwing herself into his arms, she sobbed. "This is the most incredible gift, and even though Mom can't be here with us tomorrow, I will carry her in my heart. Dad, I love you so much!"

Chapter 3

Except for my grand entry, the rehearsal dinner went off exceptionally well. When the last guest left, and only the wedding party remained, we all sat down for one last drink. And what a wedding party it was. Dakota was the best man, and now I was the maid of honor. Claudia's cousins, Tina and Debra, flew in from New York to be her bridesmaids.

Last but not least, my brother, Mark and Officer Antonio Moretti were ushers. We were a colorful group, but it was not lost on me that we were missing one very important person. Dakota would make a great best man, but everyone knew that was a role only my Josh could honestly fill.

The time had come for Claudia and me to make our way up to her room. As we opened the door, Mom and Guile were there, waiting for our arrival. They both jumped to their feet to embrace us when we came through the door.

Tears were streaming down my mother's cheeks, and she was smiling so hard it looked like her face would break. "Allie, I can't believe you are truly here."

Taking my hand, she led me over to the bed. Laying across it was a long white garment bag. "I think this belongs to you."

Spinning to face Claudia, I gasped. "What is this?"

"It's your maid of honor dress."

"What, are you kidding?"

"Would I kid about something as important as your maid of honor dress?"

"But how? I don't get it."

Dakota's father, Paco Channing, an old friend of my grandfather's, stepped out of the adjoining room. "I had faith in the stars, my dear. I saw it in a dream that you would be here. I told them to prepare. Even though they all thought I was crazy, I knew you would show."

Claudia stepped over and hugged him. "It's true. He felt so strongly about it he paid for the dress and had it delivered with mine. Even today, as the time was running short, he insisted we bring the dress and said no matter where you were, the universe would bring you here."

Moving over to him, I kissed him on the cheek and shrugged. "I don't know how this all works, but one thing I know for certain is that it is important to have faith in the universe. Somehow, there is a grand plan, and we are protected by our guides, guardian angels, or whatever you may choose to call them. Thank you for having faith, Paco."

Looking at her watch, Mom announced, "Goodness, it's almost eleven o'clock. We all need to get some sleep! The bride and maid of honor certainly can't show up to the wedding with circles under their eyes. We all have a busy and eventful day tomorrow. What do you say, Guile? Are you ready to turn in?"

"Mom, you and Guile have a room here? I mean, you have —"

She shook her head in laughter. "I guess we do have a lot of catching up to do, honey. Let's talk about all this later."

"Mom, I didn't mean —"

As she opened the door to leave, she grinned. "It's all right, Allie. I love you, honey. See you in the morning."

As soon as my mother closed the door behind her, I looked at my best friend. "Claudia, Mom and Guile?"

"Why are you so surprised? You introduced them. Well, so to speak. Your mom is not dead yet, you know!"

"I know; I guess it is just a shock. So much has changed in the past six months. What scares me, even more, is where have I been all this time? Why can't I remember anything? I feel like Rip Van Winkle, but instead of sleeping twenty years, I only slept six months. There is so much I need to figure out and so many unanswered questions. I'm not sure if my life will ever seem normal again."

"Allie, what's normal anyway? If you ask me, normal is way overrated! Seriously, I know this has got to be frightening for you. I can't begin to imagine what it would be like to get plucked out of my life, only to be plunked back into it six months later. I mean, maybe you just have to get used to a new normal!"

"Well, Claudia, you certainly are right about that. I mean, it doesn't feel like six months have passed. When I woke up late this afternoon at George's, I thought I had fallen asleep for just a few hours. I even woke up remembering a little of what I thought was a dream while I was napping. As crazy as it sounds, I am having a hard time figuring out when I am dreaming and when I'm awake or what is real and what is a dream."

"Allie, that must be so scary for you. I can't imagine feeling that way!"

"That is the strangest part; I don't feel scared, just confused."

"Hey, I know you, and I am sure you will sort this all out in time, don't you worry."

"I can't promise that I won't worry, but I can commit to letting it go long enough to enjoy one of the most important days in your life."

"That works for me, but if I am going to be a bride without bags under my eyes, we need to get some shuteye."

As we climbed into bed, I chuckled. "Well, we can't have that, can we? Hey, what time is your wedding tomorrow, anyway?"

"It's going to be a candlelight service. We're getting married at seven tomorrow evening, but I have plans for us the entire day."

"Well, I hope you allowed some time for us to sleep in a little."

"That depends on what you call sleeping in."

"Okay, give me the *Reader's Digest* version then."

"I'm not sure if there is a *Reader's Digest* version, but our day will start with breakfast at nine. We have to be at the spa by ten o'clock for manis and pedis. At eleven-thirty, we come back to our room for a light lunch at noon."

Fluffing my pillow, I buried my head in it. "You certainly have thought of everything, haven't you?"

"Wait, there's more. I've arranged for us to have a one-and-a-half-hour massage right here in our room at one o'clock."

"Claudia, we will be exhausted before the wedding even starts."

"No, we won't; I've thought of that, too. So, we have from two-thirty until four-thirty to just relax and take a nap. At four-thirty, we have an appointment at the salon to have our hair and makeup done. Then, it's back to the bridal sweet to get dressed. The limo arrives at six-thirty to take us to the church, and well, I guess you know the rest."

"Wow, Claudia, I'm so proud of you! You thought of everything, but I'm more than a little sad that I wasn't here to help you with your plans."

"To be honest, Allie, it was your mom who filled in for you as the maid of honor until you got here. She set this all up for me. I couldn't have done it without her. She was truly a godsend for me, and to be honest, I think it helped keep her mind off the fact that you weren't here to do the work. Your disappearance was extremely hard for her, but I have to say, she never gave up faith. She kept saying, 'I know Allie will find her way back to us.'"

I can't be sure which one of us passed out first, but Claudia and I talked until we both drifted off to sleep.

Chapter 4

The following morning, I slept so soundly I didn't even hear the wake-up call from the front desk. After answering it, Claudia stood in the middle of the queen-sized bed and started jumping up and down.

"Wake up! Wake up! It's my wedding day. You know I will jump up and down until you either wake up or fall out of this bed!"

"Okay, okay, enough already. Don't you think we are a little old for this game?"

"Absolutely not! Even when we get old and live in an old folks' home, I will climb up on the bed with my walker and jump until you wake up and join me for the day."

"Just what makes you think I will live with you at an old folks' home?"

"You will, and you know it. Come on, it's eight forty-five, and room service will be here at nine with our breakfast."

"That's nice, but really, Claudia, I think I just need a coffee."

"Al, we need to eat a good meal. It's going to be a long day. Besides, I ordered your favorite things: coffee, eggs Benedict, and fresh-baked Maine blueberry muffins."

"Well, that sounds great, but what, no orange juice?"

"No, I did better than that! I ordered us mimosas!"

"That sounds even better! I guess I could eat after all."

When they delivered our breakfast, we devoured our meals in record time. I had to confess. It was terrific! We were both members of the clean plate club that morning. After we demolished everything, we headed off to the spa to meet Claudia's cousins, Tina and Debra. Claudia and my mother planned an unforgettable day, jam-packed with relaxing activities. Just as Claudia had promised, we were back to the bridal suite promptly at four-thirty and had an opportunity to just sit and relax before we finished getting dressed. At five forty-five, my cell phone rang.

"Hi, Mom."

"Hey, Allie, are you almost ready?"

"We are. We have had the most amazing day. The only thing left for us to do is get into our dresses."

"That's great, honey. We'll see you at the church. I just wanted to check-in and make sure you didn't need anything. I also wanted to tell you that the gift you made for Claudia is in the nightstand drawer next to the bed."

"Mom?" I hesitated, the feeling of appreciation rising in my throat.

"Yes, honey, what is it?

"Thank you so much for helping Claudia plan this day. I'm so sorry I wasn't here for her, and it means the world to me that you were!"

"Allie, honey, I was happy to do it! Claudia is like a second daughter to me. I wouldn't have it any other way."

Ending the call with Mom, I turned to the girls. "What do you say, should we do this?"

Tina propped her hands on her hips. "Well, unless Claudia is going to make a run for it, I would say we should. What do you say, Claudia? You're not going to tuck tail and run, are you?"

"Heck no! Why would I run from the love of my life? That's just not happening, not in this lifetime anyway!"

The humor wasn't lost on me. "I don't think you would run from him in any lifetime!"

As I slid into my dress and zipped it up, I looked at Claudia's reflection behind me. "It fits like a glove, and it is the most beautiful shade of teal I think I have ever seen. Claudia, you certainly picked the perfect dress for me. It's just amazing."

Stepping closer, she stood behind me and wrapped her arms around my shoulders. "Well, it is our favorite color, and you know I know you as well as I know myself. I just knew you would love that dress! Wait until you see mine. I have a little surprise."

Smoothing my dress with my hands, I turned to Tina and Debra. "I think it's time to get this bride into her wedding gown. What do you say?"

Debra stepped over and began unzipping the garment bag. "Let's do this!" As the bag fell open, a row of teal ribbon woven into the fabric from the right shoulder of the dress to the waistline fell freely down to the hem of Claudia's wedding dress.

Tears of joy for my best friend since childhood swelled in my eyes.

Picking up the hem of my dress, I spun around, stepped over to the nightstand, and pulled out a small box from the drawer. Opening it, I lifted out a freshly pressed handkerchief that was embroidered with teal blue thread. "Here, I had one of these made for each of us a few years ago for our weddings. My mother knew about it and brought it with her yesterday to give it to you today."

"Allie, the threading is teal blue as well."

"It is. I knew you couldn't wear that old tattered shawl that Grandfather gave you, but this was meant to be a reminder that he is here with us today."

We got Claudia into her gown, and as she turned to me, I carefully picked up the veil and crown to place them on her head. After pinning them in place, I kissed her on the cheek.

"Claudia, that crown and veil fit so well together. They look like they were designed just for you. You are, without a doubt, the most beautiful bride I have ever seen. Jake is one lucky man. Just wait till he lays eyes on you! You are going to take his breath away!"

A tear leaked from Claudia's eye. "I am so unbelievably grateful that you made it here today. The day just wouldn't have been the same without you."

I reached up, wiping the tear before it could run down her cheek. "Come on now, you are going to mess up that beautiful makeup job that took over an hour to do."

There was a knock at the door, and a voice on the other side called out, "The limousine is here!"

The ride to the church was short, but each of us took a minute to share a childhood memory with Claudia.

Tina went first. "Claudia, remember when we snuck out of the house during the family reunion at Grandpas? No one ever figured out we were gone. We thought we were so grown up then. Remember? We took a few cigarettes from my mom's purse, smoked them, and we were so sick after that; I know for sure that was what cured me from ever wanting to try to smoke again."

Debra piped in. "You were the only one that got sick! I think you were the only one that actually inhaled the smoke. I have a better story than that. Remember when we went to Indian's Last Leap in Springvale? If our parents ever knew we went there to swim, they would have grounded us for life."

Feeling perplexed, I responded, "Claudia, you never told me those stories."

"That's right, you would have called me a rabble-rouser and wouldn't have hung around with me. We could never have become best friends."

"That's not true!"

"Oh, for crying out loud, Allie, yes, it is. You wouldn't hang around with Jeannie and Kara just because they used to sneak out and swim in the lake behind their house at night. You said they would get in trouble, and you didn't want to hang around with them because they were such a bad influence. You were such a Goody Two-shoes."

"I was, wasn't I? Well, I do recall a certain day we decided to skip school. We went to the beach, and I got the worst sunburn in my entire life."

"I know, and when you got home, you went right to your room before your mother saw you so she wouldn't see how red you were."

"See, I wasn't always a Goody Two-shoes!"

"Oh, please, Allie, that was senior skip day. All the parents expected us to skip that day. I bet your mother knew and just never said anything."

The limo pulled up in front of the church. Taking Claudia's hand, I smiled. "This is it, my friend, you're going in there as Claudia Buchanan and coming out as Claudia Carpenter."

"No, not quite."

"What do you mean by that?"

"I'm coming out as Claudia Buchanan-Carpenter."

"That's just semantics. You know what I meant!"

At six-fifty, we all got out of the car, climbed the stairs, and entered the back of the church. Claudia's father was there waiting, and when he laid eyes on her, he smiled. "Well, hello, my little princess. Are you ready to do this?"

"Yes, Daddy, I am."

"Daddy? You haven't called me that since you were knee-high to a grasshopper!"

"You will always be Daddy to me, just like I will always be your little princes."

Right on cue, at seven o'clock, the organist started playing the music for the wedding to begin. Tina began down the aisle first, followed by Debra and then me. When we stepped upon the altar and turned, the doors at the back of the church swung open. The wedding march began playing as the guests stood and turned to see Claudia and her father enter the chapel.

Stopping just in front of the altar, Claudia's father lifted her veil off her face, which revealed the beautiful crown he had designed just for her. He pulled his handkerchief out of his pocket to wipe a tear from his eye, and then placed her hand in Jake's as they helped her step up to meet him. As she turned to me, I took her flowers, and the minister began.

"I would like to thank everyone for being here this evening on this joyous occasion."

Suddenly, something on the balcony at the back of the church caught my attention. All the hairs on the nape of my neck rose, and closing my eyes as tightly as I could, I prayed. "Please, please, don't let anything spoil this day for Claudia."

Despite my fear, I slowly gazed up to see if there was someone there. Much to my relief, it was Detective Payne entering the balcony from the back stairwell. Although

Claudia invited him, she told me he was not attending the wedding as a guest, but he was on duty that day. Payne had staffed a security detail for the event and was there, heading up the group. He looked down at me and smiled, giving me a thumbs up.

I had a hard time staying focused during the ceremony. I just couldn't seem to shake the feeling of impending doom. Something was off. Something was not quite right. Although I couldn't put my finger on it, there was a lingering, looming feeling over us that made me extremely uncomfortable.

My mind continued to wander until I heard the minister say, "I now pronounce you husband and wife. Jake, you can now kiss your bride."

Everyone stood and began clapping as the organist started playing, and the newly married couple took their leave to the back of the chapel.

After the photo shoot outside the church, Guile drove my mother and the wedding party back to the reception in Dakota's Hummer limousine. Popping open a bottle of champagne, Dakota proposed a toast. "Let's all raise our glasses to the newly married couple. May they live in bliss for many years to come."

We all raised our glasses as my brother, Mark, added, "Yes, here is to our cherished friends, Claudia and Jake."

When we arrived back at the York Harbor Inn, the wedding party entered a beautiful large room to join the newlyweds for another photo opportunity while the guests arrived at the reception hall.

At eight o'clock sharp, the wedding planner entered the room. "Okay, everyone, it's time to line up to enter the reception where we will officially introduce Claudia and Jake as a married couple for the first time.

Dakota looked over and reached out for my hand. "Shall we?"

"There is no time like the present."

The wedding party lined up outside of the reception hall, waiting for our cue to enter.

Dakota looked at me and smiled. "Look, Allie, it's not lost on me that we are missing a very important person here tonight, but for Claudia's sake, I am thrilled you made it back to us on time."

"Thank you, Dakota."

We entered the reception hall as the deejay announced, "Here are our best man and maid of honor, Mr. Dakota Channing and Ms. Allie Callahan." While we made our way to our seats at the head table, he continued. "And now, folks, I have the honor of announcing, for the very first time, the bride and groom, Mr. Jake Carpenter and Mrs. Claudia Buchanan-Carpenter. Please welcome them!"

Everyone stood as they made their way into the room.

Within ten minutes, servers were serving the meal. Dakota turned to me. "Hey, Allie, what do you say that after the wedding, I give you a ride back to the Summit?"

"Thank you. That would be great since I don't have a car. In fact, I am not even sure if I still have an apartment."

With a bit of hesitation and caution in his voice, Dakota whispered, "What do you say we save that discussion for the ride home?"

"Sure, I guess we should just try to enjoy the evening."

The tapping of silverware on stemware cut our conversation short, and then the deejay announced, "I think it's time to get our bride and groom up here to have their first dance as husband and wife so we can get this party rolling."

The entire evening was a huge success. When it was time for Claudia and Jake to leave, everyone lined up to make a tunnel for them to run through. Before they headed out, Claudia turned to me. "Allie, this was the most magical day of my life. I am so grateful you made it back to share it with me. I love you like a sister, and that will always be true."

I reached out and hugged her as hard as my arms would allow. "That goes for me, too. I can't imagine missing this day for the world. I love you, sis. That is what you have always been to me and will always be to me. Enjoy your life with that great husband of yours. He's one of the good guys!"

"You aren't kidding! I got lucky with this one!"

"Yes, you did! See you when you both get back."

The words no sooner left my lips, and I had a horrible sinking feeling. As she walked away, I pulled her back. "Claudia, have a safe trip!"

"I will, no worries! We're not even going that far. We're spending the week in Conway, New Hampshire. Stay out of trouble until we get back, will ya?"

Chapter 5

That evening, as they left the reception, Jake gazed up. "Look at that amazing sky. The stars are so bright. They must be shining just for us tonight!"

Claudia stepped out into the parking lot and raised her arms. "It is our ancestors sending us messages of joy from the ages!"

Jake caught up to her and swept her up in his arms. "All right then, if that's the case, let's keep this celebration going."

They got in the car and headed out, but neither spoke a word during the first fifteen minutes of the ride.

Jake finally broke the silence. "Claudia, are you okay?"

"Yes, of course!"

"Why are you so quiet, then? Are you having second thoughts about us leaving for our honeymoon?"

"Of course, not. I am really excited about it, but I have to admit I am a little concerned that we aren't with everyone, keeping an eye on things regarding Allie."

"Do you want to go back? I can return to work and tell Payne we are going to postpone this trip for a couple of months."

"Are you kidding? We are definitely not going to let anything get in the way of this amazing honeymoon we've planned."

She no sooner got the words out of her mouth when Jake took a left turn off the main road. Claudia reached over and nudged Jake's shoulder. "This is not the right turn. You still have a way to go."

"Oh, this is a shortcut."

"No, it's not. You need to get back on Route 109."

"Trust me, Claudia, this is right."

She smiled. "Okay, if you say so. I would hate to have to say I told you so."

Without her knowledge, Jake had something special planned for their wedding night and the first day of their honeymoon. Not long after he left the main road, he pulled off to the side next to the entrance of a breathtaking location, lit up by a canopy of bright stars and the most beautiful autumn moon they had ever seen.

Without saying a word, he turned to Claudia, smiled, and continued pulling the car into the bottom of a long gravel driveway, putting it in park. Getting out, he walked around, opened Claudia's car door, and walked her over to a parked, running golf cart.

A woman standing next to it reached out to shake their hands. "Good evening! Welcome to Tuckaway Tree Farm. You're right on time! I'm Lynn Park and I am here to welcome and escort you up to your lodging for the evening."

They climbed into the golf cart and as Lynn drove them up the dirt road to their honeymoon retreat, Claudia looked over to Jake. "It's just perfect! It's everything I could have imagined and more."

On the hill was a circular building made of lattice and poles covered in fabric.

As they pulled up, Jake turned to Claudia. "This is what they call a yurt, honey."

Lynn brought their bags into the yurt and then excused herself and left.

Claudia and Jake stepped back outside on the deck. As they looked out over the landscape, there were hundreds of evergreen trees planted in neat rows across the field. Claudia curled up into Jake's arms. "A Christmas tree farm and retreat. This is just amazing. What a beautiful place to spend our first night as husband and wife."

Jake opened the door, swept Claudia in his arms, and carried her across the threshold into the expansive living quarters. Although the evening was cool, Lynn had made a fire in the woodstove that lit the room in a soft romantic way, engulfing them in an extraordinarily warm and cozy hug.

Claudia squeezed Jake's neck and kissed him on the cheek. "This is the most romantic thing anyone has ever done for me!"

Placing her down on her feet, he wrapped his arms around her waist and looked into her eyes. "Buckle up, my dear. You are going to have a whole life of romance like this. I promise."

"Jake, can we celebrate all our anniversaries here?"

"If that is what you want, that is what we'll do."

"I love you so much, Jake! What did I ever do to deserve to be this happy?" Taking Jake by the hand, Claudia sighed. "I think it is way past the time to consummate this union. I don't think I can wait one more second."

Chapter 6

As Dakota and I were driving home, the gravity of what my life would look like from now on began weighing on me. The joy and excitement of Claudia's wedding was a healthy distraction, but now the reality of what I was going to face was quickly sinking in.

The car was eerily silent, and neither of us said a word until we pulled up to the entrance of the Summit. Dakota broke the silence. "Allie, I think you should join me in the penthouse so we can talk."

"That's a great idea. I have a feeling there are a lot of things you may need to tell me, starting with, if I still have an apartment or not."

Guile greeted the car and opened my door. "Welcome home, Allie. Your mom is waiting in the lobby for you. She wanted to be here to help you tonight."

"Thank you so much, Guile. That's the best news ever."

As I entered the Summit, I was so relieved to see my mother waiting.

"Hello, Allie. How are you holding up, honey?"

Grinning, I kissed her on the cheek. "Better than I could have imagined under the circumstances."

A look of peace washed over her face. Sighing a breath of relief, she took me in her arms. "You are by far one of the bravest people I have ever known. You definitely take after your father in that respect."

"You are the second person to say that to me in the past couple of days, but the truth is, I think I am just growing used to all the strange, as well as the amazing things that are happening to me now. I guess I would just say that I have learned to trust in the wisdom of the universe and roll with all the punches that it can dish out."

Dakota came through the door. "I'm sorry for the interruption, but why don't we all go up to the penthouse and get settled in. I think we have a lot to talk about." He turned to the front desk. "Sandy, please hold all my calls this evening. Take a message and say that I will be unavailable until noon tomorrow."

"Certainly, sir."

"Thank you."

As we stepped out of the elevator into the penthouse, Dakota asked us to take a seat. "Can I get anyone something to drink? Perhaps a nightcap, soda, or even a coffee?"

My mother spoke first. "I would love a coffee if it's not too much trouble."

"No trouble at all. I have a Keurig coffee maker. In fact, why don't you join me in the kitchen so you can pick out a flavor? I have several."

"I would love to. Would anyone else like a coffee while we're at it?"

Guile and I both raised our hands.

"Alrighty then, two more coffee's coming up."

"I'll just have a regular coffee, Mom, with cream only. No flavored coffee for me."

Guile smiled. "You know how I like mine, honey."

As Dakota and Mom left the room, I turned to Guile. "You know how I like mine, honey?"

A colossal look of worry came over his face at my remark. "Oh, I am truly sorry, Allie. I forgot this is all so new to you."

I waved my hand at him. "Are you kidding? I am so happy for you both. You have obviously been busy getting to know each other while I was missing in action."

We had long conversations that evening about what I had missed while I was away. I learned Jake moved in with Claudia. My mom and Guile had taken their relationship to the next level. They weren't married, but she joked they were living in sin. I also found out that because Dakota had not found a suitable tenant for the penthouse, he leased it to them, and that was where they were living now.

I had taken in as many changes as I believed I could handle. "Mom, since I don't have an apartment anymore, do you think I could crash at your place?"

"Why, of course, honey. Let's go over and get you set up and into your room. We can talk some more tomorrow."

"Thank you, that sounds great!"

Mom kissed Guile on the cheek. "I'll see you in a while, take your time."

"I'll be right there."

Chapter 7

The following morning, I woke up to the smell of brewing coffee and fresh muffins in the oven. Getting up, I threw on a robe and went to the kitchen to find my mother fumbling through the morning paper that was sprawled out on the counter.

Reaching into a cabinet above her head, she handed me a mug. "Good morning, honey. How are you feeling this morning?"

"Honestly, I feel a bit of jet lag. Maybe I flew here from some exotic location before I lost my memory of the past six months."

"Very funny!"

I poured myself a coffee and joined her at the counter. "Anything interesting happening in the news?"

"No, not really, but they're going to have a fundraiser for the food bank at the Stanford Junior High School gym next month. I heard there was an article in the paper this morning with all the details and I was just looking for it. Do you think you might like to volunteer with me on that? I helped them last year, and it was a great success."

"I don't know, Mom. I'm not so sure I want to get involved in anything like that until things settle down."

"That's okay; I just thought it might be a pleasant distraction as you work on figuring things out."

I got up from the table and went to the oven. "Are the muffins done?"

"They might be. Check them and see."

Guile walked into the kitchen. "Allie, your mother always knows how to get me up in the morning. All she has to do is throw something delicious in the oven, and it draws me out of bed.

Taking the muffin tin out of the oven and waving it in front of his face, I snickered. "That is one of her oldest tricks. That's how she used to get Mark and me up every morning for school when we were kids."

I put the muffins on a dish and placed them on the table. "Mom, speaking of Mark, I was contemplating going into the office today to see how things are going there. I think I should at least check-in to see if I can contribute in some way after being gone and out of the loop for so long."

"That's probably a good idea. I know your apprentice, Tara, has been working on some new marketing plans for a company you picked up at the end of last year. I think the name of it is Organic Gardens."

"That's great! That's a market we haven't worked in yet. She's incredible, and I am sure she is up to the task. I can't wait to see what she is putting together."

After breakfast, I excused myself and went to shower. As I left the kitchen, my mother called out, "Allie, Dakota called about a half-hour ago and offered to let you use his convertible today. Actually, he said you were welcome to use it until you had a chance to pick up your car."

I stopped and turned just outside the doorway. "Really? That is extremely generous of him. To be honest, I hadn't even thought to ask where my car was."

"We put it in storage, honey. I hope you don't mind."

"That's fine. I was thinking about trading it in any way. Maybe we could pick it up later in the week and visit a couple of car dealers. I think a new car might help me move on a little. The process of choosing and buying one would be a good distraction at the very least."

"Sure, that sounds great. What do you say we plan to do just that, maybe Wednesday?"

"Wednesday would be perfect. Maybe we can have lunch together somewhere before we go car shopping."

Forty-five minutes later, I was in the car and headed to the office. Suddenly, it occurred to me that it would be a good idea to stop by to check-in with Detective Payne. I pulled up and parked in front of the station. Sitting there for a few minutes, I contemplated whether I really wanted to make this visit. Would he have news about Josh's disappearance?

After all, it had been several months. Maybe there were some new developments. So, this was it. I was going in, and as I walked through the doors, I was a little surprised that I didn't recognize the woman at the front desk. She was just one more change that served as a reminder of how long I had been gone.

"Hello, how can I help you?"

"Hi, I am here to see Detective Payne. Is he available?"

"Let me check, and your name?"

"My name is Allie Callahan."

As she paused, a large grin came across her face. Reaching out over the desk, she offered her hand. "Wow, so you're the infamous Allie Callahan. It's such an honor to meet you. My name is Stacy Anderson. Please have a seat. I'll call Detective Payne. I am sure he will want to see you!"

Payne entered the lobby two minutes later. "Hello, Allie, am I glad to see you. We have been so worried. Please come down to my office so we can talk." He turned to the front desk. "Stacy, I don't want any interruptions while I'm meeting with Allie. Please forward my calls to voicemail."

"Absolutely."

As we entered his office, he motioned for me to sit in the chair in front of his desk. "Allie, first let me say how grateful we all are to have you home safe and sound. We have been working around the clock trying to figure out what the hell happened to you. If you don't mind my asking, where have you been?"

"No, I don't mind your asking, but I am not sure you'll like the answer."

"I have no doubt, but just try me anyway!"

"All right, here goes! As far as I'm concerned, I was only gone for the weekend."

"What?"

"Yes, in my reality, I left this past Friday to head up to George's farm for some rest and relaxation. I stayed for three days and returned on, what I believed, was Monday evening. When I finally got a chance to speak with my family and friends, I learned it was actually Saturday evening. That wasn't the worst of it, though. Not only was it a Saturday, but it was six months later. So, I guess my real answer to you is that I don't know where I was all that time. I do remember a few things I thought were a dream when I woke up at George's late in the afternoon on Saturday. Well, I think it was a dream. I'm never quite sure anymore. Besides that, the rest of the time is totally lost to me."

"Damn, I would like to say I'm surprised, Allie, but as we both know from past experience, your life doesn't seem to follow the expected norms."

"I know, but I believe there has to be a reason this is all happening. Last night when I went to bed, I couldn't sleep. I couldn't stop thinking about the time I spent at George's farmhouse. I kept playing the events of my weekend over and over in my mind to no avail."

As the words left my lips, I saw something out of the corner of my eye. I turned to look, but there was nothing there. It must have been written all over my face because Payne immediately reacted.

"Allie, what is it?"

"Ah… I'm not sure." I saw it again directly behind him and instantly had a vague recollection of something that happened over my weekend at the farm.

"Allie, what is it? You look like you just saw a ghost."

"Not exactly; I think it was more like an apparition."

"What?"

"Do you remember, after I was attacked in my office, I kept seeing that little girl in a hospital gown?"

"How could I forget? It seemed she would always show up to warn you about something."

"I just now remembered something about her. While I was at George's, she appeared to me. At first, I thought I was dreaming, but then we spoke. She told me she was visiting me to help me remember my gifts, of which I guess there are many."

"Who is she? Did you figure that out?"

"That's the crazy thing. I didn't even recognize her, but she told me she was me from my youth."

"What? Wait, I don't understand."

"I don't understand entirely either, but she said the reason I didn't recognize her is that the circumstances of my life had covered my eyes to the truth, and it was past time for me to embrace my gifts. She told me that, then, and only then, would I recognize who I was in my youth and who I was to be in my future."

"Is that who you just saw?"

"No, but that is a story for another time. Let me sort this all out first."

"Really? You can't just leave me hanging like that!"

"All I can say is that I think it is one of my ancestors. My great-grandmother, to be exact. I believe she may be here to help me move forward. We'll see."

"Why doesn't that surprise me?"

"I guess you are getting used to the oddities of my existence, just like I am. Enough about me. I came to check in with you to see if you had any more information regarding Josh's disappearance."

"I would have to say that I have good news on that front and some not-so-good news."

"Well, give me the not-so-good news first."

When Payne went on to deliver the not-so-good news, he appeared to be twisted up in a tight knot. "That would be that there haven't been any breakthroughs in your case. But the good news is that we have put a team together to reexamine all the evidence. They're going to begin first thing tomorrow morning."

"Do you think I could assist the team with that review?"

"No, Allie, I am going to tell you the same thing I told Jake. If there is something we need from either of you, we will ask, but you are both too close to this case personally to be involved. I promise, if I think you can be of assistance, I will call you in."

"I guess I can live with that."

With some hesitation in his voice, he continued, "Good; however, if you're interested, there is something else I wanted to talk to you about."

"Oh really? And what might that be?"

"Just before you went up to George's for the weekend, the mayor approached me about hiring you as a consultant here at the station."

"Consultant?"

"Yes, we have put together a new task force for cold cases. He felt with your, and I quote, 'Many special talents,' you would be an excellent addition to that team."

"Ah, I don't exactly know what to say to that."

"Take some time to think about it. I don't need an answer right away. We can talk terms at a later date if you choose to move forward with us."

"I'll do that. I am on my way to see Mark at the office and check in with him this afternoon, but I'll get back with you in the next couple of days."

Leaving the station, I headed over to meet with my brother, only to discover they were functioning just fine without me. I stepped into his office. "Hi, Mark, it looks like Tara has filled my shoes here quite well."

"You have some big shoes to fill, but when you promoted her and started assigning her accounts, you made an excellent choice."

"I'm glad you feel that way because I want to run something by you."

"Uh, oh! I'm not sure I like the sound of that. What's

going on, Allie?"

"I'm thinking of a change."

"A change? What kind of change?"

"What would you say if I told you that Payne has asked me to work as a consultant on a new task force for cold cases?"

"But, Allie, what about the firm?"

"That's just it, you have everything running so smoothly here, and you certainly have done just fine without me for the past several months."

"Well, I am not sure I would say just fine."

"Look, Mark, I can continue to work as a board member and keep my hand on the pulse of things here. You can certainly call me when you feel you can use my assistance, but I think this is a direction I would like to go in. I see an opportunity to make a real difference in the lives of many people by helping out in this way."

"I get it, Allie. I guess you need to do what you think is best. As long as you promise you will be just a phone call away!"

"You know me, Mark, I won't let you down."

Chapter 8

That same morning, when Jake woke up in their little honeymoon getaway, Claudia was gazing out the window. Raising on one elbow, he studied her as she looked out over the field of Christmas trees. She was wearing only his tux shirt and had a steaming mug of coffee in her hands. The bright sunlight danced off her long hair that gracefully flowed down over her shoulders.

Breaking the silence, he gasped. "God, you are so beautiful, Claudia. How did I ever get through my life before you became a part of it?"

As Claudia turned toward the bed, the sun's light shone through her shirt, making her shapely body just slightly visible through the fabric. "Well, Mr. Carpenter, I think you didn't know any better before you met me. After all, you can't miss something you have never experienced. The real question is, what could you ever do without me in your life from now on? I know I could never imagine my life without you in it."

Patting his hand on the mattress, he motioned for her to join him. "Hey, enough of this mushy stuff. I have lots of plans for the day, but before we get on with them, Mrs. Claudia Buchanan-Carpenter, what do you say?"

"Oh, I do like the way that sounds! So just what are your plans, anyway?"

"Well, come over here, and I'll tell you all about them!"

"Oh no, you don't, Mr. Carpenter. I have another idea. What do you say we get dressed and take a stroll around this beautiful tree farm? If I join you over there, I'm afraid we will never get any of your plans accomplished today."

In protest, he agreed, climbed out of bed, and they were out strolling around the property within the hour. The scenery took their breath away as they walked down through the parade of Christmas trees.

Approaching the edge of the field, Claudia hesitated. "Jake, listen. Do you hear that?"

"Hear what? It's pretty quiet out here, honey."

"Yes, I know, but stop and just listen." She pointed into the woods. "Don't you hear the brook?

Claudia grabbed Jake's hand. "Come on!"

As they entered the tree line and came up over a slight incline, there it was.

Jake laughed. "Well, I'll be darned. Good ears!"

"Hey, Jake, what do you say we come here this Christmas and cut down our very first Christmas tree? This is such a wonderful place."

"I think that's a great idea. When I called to make our reservation, the owners, Sue and Lynn, sent me a brochure. At Christmas, when they sell trees, they open a little gift shop and sell things they have made by hand from wood. They also hold special events and weddings here. Maybe we could renew our vows in a few years and host a party here for our friends and family."

"I love that idea, you're on!"

After spending the morning in the sun and hiking around the tree farm, enjoying the beautiful landscape, Claudia and Jake went back to the yurt to pack and head to Conway. As they got in the car, Jake teased, "So, Mrs. C, are you ready for our next adventure?"

"Why yes, I am, Mr. C."

They found their way back to Route 109. Passing through Stanford, Claudia couldn't help notice the park where she always went jogging with Allie was decorated for the holidays. "They seem a little early with the decorations this year."

"I see that, but I'm not surprised." Pointing to the far side of the park, he smiled. "They put up a hut for Santa this year, and I heard they are going to have him here the day after Thanksgiving."

Like a little kid, the excitement welled up in Claudia. "That will be so crazy! Can we come and visit the park that evening when it is all lit up? I would love to get some photos for a series of paintings I'm planning. Can we?"

He chuckled. "Why, your wish is my command, Mrs. C."

A few miles down the road, Jake pulled into an apple orchard. "What do you say, should we pick some apples?"

The orchard was teeming with children, running around, pulling little red wagons filled to the brim with apples they had picked. A mobile food vendor was selling hot cider, caramel apples, hot dogs, and apple crisp. As they drove into the parking area, a hay wagon pulled by a large tractor was coming up the hill. The children laughed and were still singing "Old MacDonald" as the wagon pulled to a stop to disembark.

"Okay, Jake, I want to do it all. I want to pick apples, ride in the hay wagon, and most of all, I want to eat all these fall treats until I can't fit one more thing in my belly."

It was nearing three o'clock when Claudia and Jake climbed into the wagon to go off on the apple orchard hayride.

"Jake, this is such a beautiful fall day. What a great idea to spend our honeymoon locally. The foliage is so beautiful this time of year, and this crisp cool air is so exhilarating."

As the tractor-pulled wagon moved through the woods that donned vibrant hues of golds and reds, Claudia pulled out her phone and snapped picture after picture to capture the grandeur that would surely be the inspiration for paintings to document their blissful honeymoon.

The wagon came to a stop at a clearing at the edge of the woods. When Claudia and Jake looked out over the hill, they could see the tops of several mountains in the distance, including Mount Washington.

"Hey, Jake, do you think we could go skiing this winter?"

"Only if you are willing to teach me how."

"Are you for real? Are you saying you have never skied? How can anyone live for any amount of time near these beautiful mountains and not?"

"I would love to learn, honey."

"All right, I am going to hold you to that!"

"I think when this ride is over, we should head out and make our way to check in at the bed-and-breakfast. What do you think?"

"Sounds like a plan to me."

At five o'clock, they arrived at the Darby Field Inn in Conway, New Hampshire. As they walked into the lobby, the woman behind the desk greeted them.

"Good afternoon. How can I help you?"

"Hello, we have a reservation under the name Jake Carpenter."

"Of course, welcome! My name is Maria, and I am one of your hosts here at the Inn. My husband, Marc, and I are honored to have you here. Your room is ready, and I believe you also have a dinner reservation in our dining room at seven o'clock, correct?"

"Yes, we do."

A gentleman walked in, moving toward the fireplace to add some logs. "Well, there's Marc now."

She called out, "Marc, honey, these are the newlyweds, Jake and Claudia. Could you please help them to their room?"

"Certainly! It's nice to meet you both, and we are so happy that you decided to spend your honeymoon at our little Inn. Please, let me show you to your quarters."

Claudia and Jake followed him up a staircase and down the hall.

"This is your room." He opened the door. "I know you didn't ask for one of our suites, but Maria insisted. This is our Mount Washington Suite. She thought you would love the panoramic mountain view and the cozy fireplace."

Claudia stepped in first. The room was warm, inviting, and featured a king-sized bed with lots of plump puffy pillows. The fireplace in the room was lit and flanked by two large, comfortable armchairs. Between the chairs was a table that held a beautiful vase of lavender flowers, a bottle of red wine, and two elegant stemmed glasses. "It is just perfect. It looks like it should be a picture in a travel magazine."

Marc set their bags down just inside the door. "Well, I guess Maria chose the right room for you. We will see you tonight at dinner. I left a menu on the nightstand with a list of the entrees we are serving this evening."

Handing Marc an envelope, Jake smiled. "That's perfect, and here, this is for you."

"No, that isn't necessary."

"Please, I insist, and thank your wife, Maria, for arranging this room for us. It was very kind of her."

After Jake and Claudia picked the straw off their clothes and out of their hair from the afternoon hayride, they got showered and went down for dinner.

The meal was superb and featured some of New Hampshire's incredible seasonal specialties. They started with a cup of New England clam chowder. The salads were served with pumpkin bread, that had a drizzle of maple syrup butter. The entrée was baked lobster pie made with fresh Maine lobster. And of course, their dessert was apple pie a la mode, baked with fresh picked apples.

After dinner, the minute they walked back into the room, Claudia wrapped her arms around Jake's neck, stared up into his eyes, and whispered, "If this is a dream, please don't wake me up. It feels like we are living in a fairytale. You're the prince and I am the princess."

"Well, isn't that what you are? Isn't that what your dad has been trying to tell you all your life?"

"Yes, but I never really felt like one until now. I love you, Mr. Jake Carpenter."

"I love you, too. I say we break open the wine and toast to many more nights like this! What do you think?"

"I say let me get into something more comfortable, and we can do just that. I had something to wear last night, but I never had a chance to put it on."

"Oh really, Mrs. C?"

"Yes, really!"

While Jake opened the bottle of wine, Claudia went to change. When she finally emerged from the bathroom, Jake's jaw dropped. "My, my, Mrs. C! If we weren't married, I would say you were planning on being a very, very bad girl! That is certainly not befitting a princess!"

"How do you know what is fitting for a princess? I'm a princess, not a nun."

After their wine, Jake picked up Claudia and placed her gently on the bed. Climbing in behind her, they sank into each other's arms and made love until they were too exhausted to even move.

Chapter 9

In the morning, the newlyweds were still sleeping off their previous evening of bliss.

When Claudia finally woke up, she couldn't believe how late it was. Rolling over, giving Jake a gentle shove, she whispered, "Hey, wake up! The morning's half over!"

Groaning and opening his eyes, he squinted. "What time is it?"

"It's already ten o'clock, and I am sure we missed breakfast downstairs."

"It's okay. We can go out in town and get a coffee and something to eat at one of the little cafés."

She whined, as only Claudia could do. "No, Jake, not if we don't get up right now! I don't want to miss a minute of our time here. There is so much for us to do, and we have lots more memories to make this week." Come on, please? Let's get up and go out and do something to reminisce about!"

Sitting up at the edge of the bed, he stretched to help wake his muscles. He suddenly sprinted to the bathroom. "Okay, you're right. I bet I can beat you to the shower?"

Claudia sprinted after him. "That's not fair, Jake Carpenter. You didn't even give me a fair warning."

Beating her into the shower, he burst out laughing. "You know what they say, all is fair in love and war?"

Claudia turned on her heels. "Oh, yeah? Well, I'll be right back."

"Claudia, where the heck are you going?"

She grabbed the ice bucket from the nightstand and bounded into the bathroom, dumping leftover ice and water in the bucket over the shower door. "Well, Mr. Carpenter, I am declaring war!"

"Oh, my God, Claudia, that was freezing cold!" He picked up and waved a white face cloth. "Truce, truce! I surrender!"

Showered and dressed, they headed out to get something for breakfast. Claudia and Jake didn't go far when they found a charming little place with outdoor seating. "Jake, if I go in and get us coffee and something to eat, will you find us a table out here on the patio? Possibly a table in this nice warm sunlight."

"Sure thing, that sounds like a good deal."

"What do you want to eat?"

"I don't know. Why don't you surprise me?"

"Surprises I'm good at. I can certainly do that!"

"Oh, yes you can. You proved that this morning in the shower."

With a rascally smile on her face, Claudia kissed Jake on the cheek. "That'll teach you not to mess with me, Mr. C."

When she stepped into the café, she was delighted with the smell of freshly baked pastries wafting from the ovens and just prepared coffee, still brewing in their pots. She walked up to the counter.

"What can I get you this fine morning?"

"What would you recommend?"

"To be truthful, that's a tough call, but I must say this time of the year, we do make a great pumpkin cheese Danish."

"All right, I'll take two of those and two cups of coffee, please, cream only."

"Is this to go, or are you eating here?"

"We are going to eat at one of your tables outside in that beautiful sunlight."

After paying, Claudia picked up the tray and headed out. She stopped in the doorway to see where Jake was sitting. He was at a table outside in the corner of the patio. She lifted the tray to signal to him, but he had the strangest blank expression on his face.

As she moved closer, she could see something red trickling down the side of his cheek. Dropping the tray of food, she ran to him as he fell face down on the table. When she kneeled beside him, he fell from his chair, knocking her to the ground. Sitting up with his head in her lap, she screamed. "Oh, my God! Help, please, somebody, help!"

In seconds, there was a crowd forming around them.

"Please, let me through. I'm a doctor. Please, get back and give us some space."

A pool of blood was already covering the ground as the doctor took off his sweatshirt and placed it under Jake's head.

Another gentleman lifted Claudia from behind and pulled her back. "Here, give the doctor some room. Are you all right, Miss?" Seeing how distraught she was, he wanted to draw her attention away from Jake. "Hey, my name is Jerry. What's your name?"

When Claudia didn't respond, he gently turned her face toward him. "Miss, can you tell me your name?"

As the doctor tore off his tee-shirt and began wrapping it around Jake's head to slow down the bleeding, he started giving instructions. "Hey, Jerry, it's Jerry, right?

"Yes."

"Jerry, I'm Dr. Stroble. She's going into shock. You need to lay her down and elevate her feet. Take off your coat and wrap her in it and try to keep her warm."

When the EMTs arrived on the scene, they were surprised to see the doctor there already working with the patients.

"We need to get this guy transported immediately. Is there a second ambulance on the way here?"

"Yes, they're right behind us."

"Okay, let's get this guy loaded up. I'll stay with you in the ambulance until we get him to the ER. Jerry, will you please stay with this woman and fill in the other EMTs? They are pulling up now."

"Sure thing, Doc."

Chapter 10

That same morning, when I woke up, I headed over to the station to have another conversation with Detective Payne. I was seriously considering his offer. After all, I enjoyed working with him and Jake in the past. It would also allow me to be around the station more, just in case something broke on my case. I would never rest until we found out what happened to Josh.

I got to the police station about twelve-thirty. Stacy was at the desk. "Hello, Ms. Callahan. How are you today?"

"I'm great, and you?"

"Good, thank you for asking."

"Can you see if Detective Payne might have time to talk to me?"

"Oh, I'm sure he does. When he came in this morning, he told me he hoped you would come by today. Let me call up to his office to see if he can see you now."

Picking up her phone, she dialed his extension. "Hello, Detective Payne, Allie is here to see you." She paused for his response and nodded. "Will do." Replacing the phone in its cradle, she looked at me with a smile. "He said you know where his office is and to send you right up."

"Okay, thank you."

I went directly to Payne's office. He was on the phone but waved for me to come in.

"Yes, he is one of ours. No, I am coming personally. I should be there in about an hour." As he hung up, he pulled his jacket off of the hook behind his desk. "Come on, Allie, you and I are taking a little ride."

"What's going on?"

"Come on, I will tell you about it on the way."

"But—"

"Allie, we need to get rolling. Come on."

I followed him down the hallway, and as we passed Stacy, he called out, "I am going to be gone for the day. Please take messages and refer any emergency calls to Officer Antonio Moretti."

She didn't even have a chance to respond as we were out the door.

Payne unlocked the squad car and we both got in. He turned on the lights and sped off. That heavy feeling of dread was coming over me again.

"Payne, where are we headed, and why am I with you?"

"We're going to Conway, New Hampshire."

"Oh, my God, it's Claudia and Jake, isn't it?"

Realizing he needed to give me a chance to absorb what he was about to say, he pulled over. "I'm sorry. I should have stopped to talk to you first. I just think I will need you on this one."

"Just tell me, is it them?"

"Yes. I don't know any of the details, but there's been a shooting. What I do know is they have both been taken by ambulance to the hospital."

"Oh, my God! I knew the day of the wedding, something was coming. I couldn't put my finger on it, but I had this sinking feeling. I didn't trust my instincts. How could I? I couldn't even remember the past six months of my life. I just thought I was being paranoid or something."

"Do you still want to go to Conway with me?"

"Of course, let's go!"

The lights flashed, and the siren roared on as we headed west on Route 109 toward Spaulding Turnpike.

We made it to the Memorial Hospital in Conway within an hour. Pulling up near the emergency entrance, we got out of the car and ran through the doors, directly to the nurse's station.

Payne pulled out his badge. "Hello, I am looking for Officer Ballenger."

"Excuse me, sir, are you, Detective Payne?" asked a male voice behind us, causing us to turn around.

"Yes. Officer Ballenger?"

"No, come with me. I'll take you to him."

As he led us down the hall, he continued. "He has been waiting for you to get here and wants to take you to the scene and go over everything with you."

Reaching the lobby entrance of the emergency room, he pointed to an officer on the opposite side of the room who was talking to a young gentleman, covered with blood. "That's Officer Ballenger."

"Excuse me, Officer Ballenger?"

"Yes, but you can call me Bill. You must be Detective Payne."

"Yes, and this is Allie. Although my name is Dennis, everyone just calls me Payne. Can you tell me how Claudia and Jake are?"

"Absolutely. First, let me put your mind at ease regarding Claudia. She has no injuries, but the doctors have sedated her and are treating her for shock." He turned to the young gentleman he had been talking with. "This is Jerry. He was at the scene and assisted Doctor Stroble with Claudia."

"Dr. Stroble?"

"Yes, fortunately, he was in town and was there when this all happened. He treated Officer Carpenter at the scene."

"And how is Jake doing?"

"We haven't heard yet; he's in surgery now."

I interrupted. "Can I see Claudia?"

"Are you family?"

"Except for her father, I'm the closest thing to family she has."

"I'm sure that will be fine. Why don't you go back to the nurse's station, explain who you are, and they will let Claudia know you are here. I am sure she will want to see you."

Before I left, Payne continued to speak with Bill. "How bad is it?"

"It's not good. Your detective took a shot to the head."

"Any suspects? Did anyone see anything?"

"Nothing yet. It was a sniper shot. They are still on the scene now. Does Jake have any enemies?"

"You could say that."

"This had to be personal. To follow him and his wife on their honeymoon and try to take him out like that? Whoever this is, they must have a serious hate-on for your officer."

I interrupted. "Payne, I need to go see Claudia!"

"Of course, we'll come and get you if anything changes."

When I got back to the emergency entrance, the nurse showed me to Claudia's room. When we walked in, she was curled up in a fetal position with her back facing the door. She was so still; I could hardly see her breathing. When I moved over to the other side of the bed, dried blood covered her face and matted her hair.

"Oh, my God, are you sure she hasn't been injured?"

"No, that's her husband's blood. At the scene, she was going into shock. They treated her in the ambulance and then she was sedated by the doctor after she arrived here. We are monitoring her closely. Please have a seat next to her. She should sleep for a while. It will be good for her to have a familiar face in the room when she wakes up."

"Of course, thank you so much!"

"Look, my name is Virginia. When she wakes, please let me know. I'll be at the nurse's station right outside this door. Can I get you anything, maybe a soda or a coffee?"

"No, thank you, I'm fine."

I took a seat in the chair next to Claudia's bed. Her face was so pale, her hair was sticky from dried blood, and she looked so small laying there, all curled up.

I leaned into my best friend and whispered, "I promise, Claudia, we are going to find this guy."

Payne walked into the room. "Oh yes, we are! Enough is enough, and I won't rest until we do."

Anger sprang up from my core. "I won't either!"

"Allie, have you given any thought to my offer?"

"Yes, that's why I came to your office this morning. I wanted to let you know I was going to accept it."

"Good! I've been giving it a lot of thought, and I am considering putting you on the team that is working your case."

"Really? I thought—"

"I know what I said, but if you promise to listen to me and only work as a consultant, I have changed my mind."

"That's great. Thank you so much, Payne!"

"Look, don't make me regret this decision. You are to work in the office only. Unless it goes through me, you are not going out in the field on this one. If your intuition kicks in and you feel inclined to strike out on your own, don't. You need to keep us in the loop every step of the way."

"I will, Payne, I promise."

"Good. I'm going to assign Officer Moretti to be with you twenty-four-seven."

"I'm good with that. Let's do it!"

"I mean it, Allie. If you go out alone, even once, I will throw you on house arrest with an ankle bracelet, and you and Antonio will be stationed indefinitely at your home."

"I get it, Payne. I have no problem with that."

Although he didn't respond verbally, his body language and expression spoke loud and clear, letting me know he didn't believe me.

As he turned to leave, he reached the door and looked over his shoulder. "Okay, Allie, I'm holding you to that! Right now, I'm going to the scene with Officer Ballenger. I am counting on you to call me if there are any changes or news about Jake."

"I will. Hey, Payne, thanks again!"

Hesitating and stretching his neck from side to side, he winced. "I hope I am making the right decision on this."

"Trust me, Payne, you are."

Chapter 11

Payne and Officer Bill Ballenger arrived in Conway to find the patio of the café taped off. Most of the forensic team had moved to a building across the street.

Bill motioned to Payne. "Let's see if they have found anything else. A good portion of the team is processing the roof across the street at that brick apartment building with the hardware storefront. Officer Todd called me about an hour ago and told me they believe the shot was taken from the roof of that building."

Moving across the street, they stopped on the sidewalk. "Hey, Todd, how are things going? Have you been able to find any more evidence to support your suspicion that the shooting occurred from this building?"

"We sure have, Bill! Given the location of the bullet wound in Officer Carpenter's head, we were able to estimate the shot's trajectory. This guy is clearly a great shot, maybe ex-military or professional. What doesn't make sense is that he was extraordinarily sloppy and made it way too easy for us to confirm that the shot was indeed taken from this building. We actually found evidence that suggests the exact location he took the shot from."

"What evidence?"

"We found a shell on the street side of the roof. He must have dropped it, but given he took only one shot, he was extremely careless."

Payne stepped back toward the curb and looked up at the roof of the building. "I wouldn't be so sure of that. If the perpetrator is who I think he is, he is calculated and doesn't leave things behind unless he intends for it to be found."

Todd reached out to shake his hand. "You must be Detective Payne. Sorry about Officer Carpenter. It sounds like you have an idea about who could be good for this shooting."

"Unfortunately, I think I might. For months, Jake and I have been investigating the attempted murder of a woman named Allie Callahan. Allie is a good friend of Officer Carpenter's and his new wife, Claudia. The suspect in the case was an ex-convict named Makya Hammonds. Regrettably, Allie and Jake are not his only two victims. Ms. Callahan's fiancé went missing during a party this past New Year's Eve. Prior to that, he left a trail of victims from Los Angeles to New York City. The case is rather complex, but that is a quick summation."

As they moved down the sidewalk, Officer Ballenger stepped down off the curb into the crosswalk. "Perhaps we could go over some more of the details of that investigation later today. Todd, why don't you give me a call when you wrap things up here and then join Detective Payne and me back at my office? If you need me in the meantime, I am heading back to the hospital to see if Officer Carpenter's wife is able to talk to us yet."

Chapter 12

S till heavily sedated, Claudia was stirring about in the hospital bed. I went to the door of her room and signaled to the nurse's station, calling out as quietly as I could. "Excuse me, Virginia, I think Claudia is starting to wake up."

Getting right up from the desk, she came into the room. As she checked her vital signs, she looked up at me. "Her moving is a good sign. She may continue to be restless in her sleep, but her pulse and blood pressure are more normal now. I believe her room is almost ready, and we are going to move her upstairs as soon as we can."

"So, you are going to admit her?"

"Yes, just for twenty-four hours. Does Claudia have any family we can call to pick her up tomorrow? The only contact number we could find for her was her husband's."

"Oh, my God, that means no one has contacted her father! He lives out of state, but he was in town for their wedding. I'm not sure if he has returned home yet. I need to call him."

"You can use a phone at the nurse's station if you need to."

"No, I have my cell. I'll step out and call."

As we stepped out of the room, the nurse pointed down the hall. "There is a small waiting room just down to the right that will give you some privacy."

"Thank you, I am sure if he is still in town, he will come right away."

As I walked to the waiting room, I dialed Claudia's father's number. He answered on the third ring.

"Hello?"

"Hello, Mr. Buchanan?"

"Yes, Allie, is that you?"

"Yes, it is. Are you still in town?"

"I am. I am planning to stay for the week. My flight isn't until next weekend. What is going on? Are you all right?"

"Yes. Look, let me start by saying that Claudia is safe, but there has been an incident."

"What kind of an incident?" Panic rose in his voice. "Where is she? Where is Jake?"

"They have been admitted to the hospital in Conway, New Hampshire. Claudia was not injured, but Jake was shot, and he is in surgery. I am so sorry to have to tell you this on the phone, but I knew you would want to be here."

"Of course! I will be there as soon as I can!"

"Please, Mr. Buchanan, I am begging you, take your time. Don't get in an accident trying to get here. I am with Claudia, and if she wakes, I will let her know you are on your way."

"Of course! Allie, do they think this is connected to your case?"

"We aren't sure of anything yet, but it's looking that way."

"Have you had a chance to tell your mother?"

"No, you were my first call, but I am going to call her now. She might want to come as well."

"Allie, why don't you call her right away, and if she does, I would be more than happy to go by, pick her up, and bring her with me."

"Thank you, Mr. Buchanan. I'll do that and call you right back."

My mother answered the phone right away. "Hi, Allie?"

"Hi, Mom, are you at home?"

"Why yes, honey, what's up?"

"I'm in Conway, New Hampshire. I drove here with Payne."

"What are you doing there?"

"Mom, it's Claudia and Jake. They came here on their honeymoon. Payne got a call this morning from an Officer Ballenger, who works at the Conway Police Department. Claudia is physically fine. They have admitted her for observation, but Mom, Jake was shot!"

"Oh, my God, Allie! Is he going to be okay?"

"We don't know; he's in surgery. I haven't been able to talk to Claudia because she is sedated, so I don't know much yet. Mr. Buchanan is still in Stanford, and he is going to drive to Conway within the hour. He thought you might want to join him."

"Yes, of course!"

"Okay, when do you think you can be ready?"

"I have no plans today, and I can leave whenever he wants to."

"All right, I'll call him and let him know he can pick you up any time."

"Okay, honey, he knows I live here at the Summit, right?"

"Yes, I'm sure he does."

"All right then, give him my cell number and have him text me when he is on the way, and I'll go down to the lobby and wait there. Honey, hang in there. I'll see you shortly."

"Thank you, Mom. I love you!"

"I love you, too, dear!"

After calling Mr. Buchanan back, I headed to Claudia's room. Payne and Officer Ballenger came through the emergency room entrance and waved for me to join them in the hallway.

"Allie, is Claudia awake yet?"

"Honestly, Payne, I don't know. I left her room about twenty minutes ago to call her father, and she was still sleeping. Were you able to find anything out at the scene? Do you think it could be Makya?"

Ballenger tipped his head inquisitively. "Payne, this is Allie Callahan? I just put it together. Allie is that good friend of Jake's wife you were talking about, right?"

"Yes, but it's much more complicated than that."

Chapter 13

Down the hall, Virginia stepped out of Claudia's room. She began waving urgently for us to meet her at the door. As we got closer, I could hear Claudia sobbing. I rushed in to find her sitting up in the bed. When she saw me, she slipped into a full-blown panic.

"Allie! Oh, my God, Allie! I need to get out of here. I need to see Jake! Is he alive? Is he here in the hospital somewhere?"

Rushing to her bedside, I lowered the rails, grabbed her, and held her as tight as I could. "Claudia, you have to calm down. If you don't, they are going to have to sedate you again."

"How can I calm down? Just look at me. I am covered with Jake's blood—Allie, he was bleeding so badly!"

Loosening my grip on her and stepping back, I looked straight into her eyes. "Claudia, Jake is alive. You need to calm down so I can talk to you."

Virginia came back into the room with medication to calm Claudia down. When she saw the needle, she became even more frantic.

"No, I don't want that! I don't want to sleep. I want to know what's going on!"

"This won't make you sleep. It will just help you relax."

I raised my hand toward Virginia. "Claudia, you need to stop long enough for me to tell you what's going on. That might help you calm down, and just maybe you won't need that shot."

As I stepped back from her, I felt her body relax just slightly. Handing her a tissue from the bedside, I gathered my words. "Look, honey, just stop and listen to me. Jake is alive. He's in surgery. He was shot and has a head wound, but we don't know just how serious it is yet."

"Allie, it was horrible. I mean, one minute we were having such an amazing time, and it was just magical, and then out of nowhere, we were thrown into this hellish nightmare. We never saw it coming! It had to be Makya! He had to be just lying in wait. We should have known; things were way too quiet. You know how he loves to use the elements of shock and surprise."

Payne stepped into the room and moved toward her bed. "Hello, Claudia. This is Officer Ballenger. He called me as soon as he found Jake's ID. I'm so sorry."

Claudia took Payne by the hand. "It's Makya, isn't it?"

"Honestly, we don't really know for sure yet, but I believe the evidence will lead us there. I'm sorry, but if you are up to it, we need to ask you a few questions."

Looking over, I waved to the nurse. "Before we start this, what do you say you take that shot, Claudia? You need to take care of yourself if you are going to be of any use to Jake."

"I guess so, but I don't want to be knocked out again."

Virginia smiled. "You're on; this is just something to help you relax."

After the nurse stepped out of the room, Payne stood akimbo. "So, Claudia, can you tell me about your morning? Did you notice anything out of the ordinary?"

"No, Payne, our honeymoon was going so well. We were both so relaxed. We slept in late this morning. Well, it was late for us. We woke up about ten o'clock. I was teasing Jake that we had missed the continental breakfast where we were staying. You know how he is, though. He just rolls with the punches. His answer to that was, 'Well, let's get dressed and go out to find some coffee.'"

"So, you didn't notice anything out of the ordinary this morning before you went to have breakfast?"

"No, not that I can think of. We were only up for about an hour before we went out. When we got to the cafe, I asked Jake to pick out a place on the patio for us to sit while I went in to get our food. When I came out of the cafe, I signaled to Jake, but he had the strangest blank expression on his face. It was like he was sitting there with his eyes open, but he was unconscious. I ran over, and just as I reached him, his upper body fell forward on the table, and then he tumbled to the ground, taking me down with him. The last thing I remember was someone dragging me away from him. The rest is kind of a blur."

I stepped closer to the bed. "Claudia, I am so sorry that you are all mixed up in this. I still can't believe how brazen Makya is."

"Allie, this is not your fault. You have got to realize that!"

Drawing my attention, Payne placed his hand on my shoulder. "Claudia is right. You can't take on any of the responsibility for the recent events. In fact, we are counting on your staying focused and strong, so you can help us get this Makya guy. Believe me, I won't rest until we catch him, throw the book at him, and lock him up for the rest of his life."

There was a knock on the door as a doctor walked into the room. "Excuse me, I'm Doctor Weisfeldt. Could I have a minute with Ms. Carpenter?"

Stepping into the room, he was still wearing surgical scrubs and paper coverings over his shoes. He took off his surgical mask. "I wanted to update you on your husband's surgery. Would you prefer for me to speak to you privately?"

"No, please, it's fine! Just tell me, how did Jake's surgery go? Is he going to be okay?"

"It is too early to tell. He's in critical but stable condition. It appears that the bullet entered the skull at the side of his head and exited with minimal damage."

"What does that mean? Please, what exactly is minimal damage?"

"What I'm saying is that the bullet penetrated his skull and exited. The damage caused by its path was mostly to the bone and not to his brain tissue."

"So, does that mean he will have no brain damage?"

"We can't say that for certain yet. The blow to Jake's head by the bullet caused a severe concussion. Our first task was to stop the bleeding. Secondly, brain swelling is a concern with any head injury. It was fortunate that the scull was cracked by the blow, because it will allow room for expansion and keep the brain from being compressed until we can get the swelling under control. He is not out of the woods by any means, but we are hopeful. It will be a while before we know the extent of how the trauma will affect him physically."

"Can I see him?"

"When we move him to ICU, you will be able to see him for a few minutes. I understand you are being admitted as well. I will make sure they take you to see him before you are taken to your room."

"Thank you so much! I'm sorry, what was your name again?"

"I'm Doctor Weisfeldt and you are entirely welcome."

As the doctor headed for the door, he hesitated. "Oh, there's one more thing I think you may want to know. There was a Doctor Stroble at the café when the shooting happened. He and another gentleman, I think his name was Jerry, stepped in to help. Honestly, I think it is what saved your husband. Whoever did this, well, let's just say that those two certainly interrupted his plan to take your husband out by being there and acting so quickly."

Payne offered his hand to the doctor. "I met them in the emergency room and thanked them both. I am so grateful they were there."

Claudia looked past Payne and the doctor, and as if she had been holding her breath, she let out a gasp. "Dad, you're here. Thank God!"

Mom, Claudia's father, Bill, and I stayed at the hospital that night. The nurses brought two extra guest chairs in, and we settled in to at least try to get a little sleep. I was just drifting off when my cell phone buzzed. It was Dakota.

"Hello?"

"Hello, Allie. Where are you? I expected you back at your mother's tonight. She's not home either! Is everything all right?"

"I am so sorry, Dakota. I should have called you. We are in Conway."

"Conway? Conway, New Hampshire?" I stepped out into the hall. "Yes, there has been a horrible incident."

"What kind of incident? Isn't that where Claudia and Jake went to spend their honeymoon?"

"Yes, but something horrible has happened! Jake was shot, and they both are in the hospital here in Conway!"

"What? Are you kidding me? Do they think it was Makya? Are they okay? Does your brother know? How about George, does he know?"

"Slow down, Dakota. First, Claudia has no physical injuries, but she's quite shaken up. They are keeping her for observation. Jake was in surgery for a good part of the day. He is in ICU right now. My mother and Claudia's father, Bill, are here with us."

"What about your brother and George?"

"My mother called my brother, but we couldn't reach George. I'm a little worried about him. I left him a couple of messages, but he hasn't called back. That isn't like him at all. Do you think you could check on him and fill him in?"

"Sure. Do you want me to come to Conway? Is there anything I can do?"

"No, not right now. Why don't you call me in the morning, and I will let you know? I may need you to bring us my mother's car. I came here with Payne yesterday after he received a call from the Conway Police Department. Bill brought my mother here after I contacted them."

"I'm more than a little troubled that you haven't heard from George." There was a concerned hesitation in Dakota's voice.

"I know, it's been gnawing at me all day! I have a sense that something isn't right, but I can't quite put my finger on it. I feel like I have been kind of off my game since I woke up at his farmhouse. I have been getting these waves of concern, but even when Claudia and Jake were in danger, I didn't feel or see it coming."

The minute the words left my lips, a wave of terror sprung over me. My whole body was buzzing, and a groundswell of nausea irrupted from my gut. "Oh, my God! I think I spoke too soon. Dakota, I have the most overwhelming feeling of dread in every ounce of my body. It's like I stuck my finger in a light socket, and my whole nervous system lit up. Something is dreadfully wrong, but I don't have a clue what it is. Why am I capable of such profound things when I cannot understand, or use them when I need them most? I just don't get it; I must be missing something.

"Look, Allie, I'm coming to Conway. First, I'll retrieve your grandfather's box from the safe room so I can bring it to you. I don't know, but maybe if you have it in your possession, things will become clearer. I don't pretend to understand any of this, but you have been without it for several months. I'll go check on George, make sure he is okay, and then I'm headed your way."

"Thank you, Dakota. I really appreciate it. It's certainly worth a try."

As I stepped back into the room, Claudia rolled over to face the door. "Allie, is everything okay?"

Moving toward her, I put my finger over my lips for her to be quiet. "Claudia, do you want to take a little walk in the hall?"

"That would be great. I'm getting more than a little sore just laying in this bed."

When we stepped out of the room, Claudia looked at me. "What's going on, Allie?"

"Do you promise to stay calm?"

"Yes. I don't think it's possible to be anything but calm with this medication they've given me, floating around in my bloodstream. She laughed. "It's some pretty good stuff!"

"Well, I'm glad somebody has their sense of humor back! But seriously, something is going on. I'm not sure exactly what, but I have a sense that something is very wrong. I am especially worried about George. I've been trying to reach him all day, but he isn't returning my calls."

"What? Have you said anything to Payne?"

"No. Do you think I should?"

"Hell ya!"

"I just spoke to Dakota on the phone, and he is going to check on George now. If he can't find him or suspects anything is wrong, I'm sure he will contact Payne. After he checks on George, he's coming here and bringing my grandfather's box to me. Dakota thought having it with me might help me; anything to figure out why I am feeling so off."

A nurse came out of the room across the hall. "Are you all right, Claudia?"

"Yes, we just thought we would stretch our legs a little."

"That's a good sign. You certainly look a lot better."

"Thank you. Is there a vending machine somewhere that we can get a drink?"

Hanging her stethoscope around her neck, she pointed down the hall. "There is a nice sitting room just down on the right. If you want to head down there, I can bring you something to drink. What would you like? I have juice, coffee, soda, or hot chocolate."

With a sigh, we responded in unison. "Oh, hot chocolate!"

Chapter 14

Back at the Summit, Dakota retrieved Allie's wooden box from the safe room as soon as he got off the phone with her. Grabbing his coat and the box from the office, he called the front desk.

"Hello, Sandy, this is Dakota. Could you please ask Henry to bring my Hummer up from the parking garage?"

"Certainly, sir. What time?"

"I'm heading out now. I'll be down in less than five minutes."

A few minutes later, the elevator door opened and Dakota stepped out. "Good evening, Sandy."

"Hello, sir. Have a pleasant evening."

Henry was standing outside with the car door open, waiting for him. "Good evening, sir. Will you be long?"

"Yes, Henry. Could you please pop the trunk for me?" Placing the box in the trunk, he tapped Henry on the shoulder. "I'm headed to Conway for the evening, and I don't expect to be back until tomorrow."

Dakota drove across town and pulled into the parking lot at George's Café at ten forty-five. As he approached the entrance, the open sign was still lit in the window. Entering the café, everything seemed copasetic. The jukebox was playing. Food in the display cases had been put away for the night, but the front of the shop was empty.

Dakota called out, "George, are you here?"

A young gentleman stepped out from the back. "Hello, can I help you?"

"I'm looking for George. Is he here this evening?"

"No, I'm sorry, he's not here."

Feeling a little uneasy, Dakota stepped up to the counter. "Excuse me, but I don't think I know you. Are you new here?"

"Yes, sir, I am. I just started working here yesterday. My name is Samuel, but you can call me Sam."

"Well, Sam, where is George? It's out of the ordinary for him to not be here at the end of any shift. Aren't you supposed to be closing in a few minutes?"

"Yes, sir, at eleven o'clock. I'm not sure why George isn't here, but he told me that if he didn't get back in time, to lock up without him."

"So, I guess you don't mind if I just take a look around?"

"I'm not sure if George would like that, sir. I don't know you, and I don't think George would appreciate me letting anyone have free rein over this place."

"Excuse me, I didn't formally introduce myself. My name is Dakota Channing. I am not just a customer, but a close friend of George's. Another mutual friend of George's has been trying to reach him all day, but he hasn't returned any of their calls. I don't know you, and he has not mentioned hiring anyone recently, so you can surely understand my concern."

Sam seemed nervous. "I'm sorry, sir, but I am going to have to ask you to leave. I am closing, and I can't have anyone here when I lock up."

"Look, Sam, Samuel, or whatever your name is, I am going to just take a walk through the café. That includes the bathrooms, kitchen, office, and walk-in freezers. If I don't find anything out of the ordinary, I will leave here and let you close up. If you don't like that, you can call the police station and ask for Detective Payne. He will definitely vouch for me."

"Uh, no sir, that will be fine."

"Yeah, I thought you might feel that way!"

"Look, mister, please just look around if you have to, and leave."

After doing a sweep of the shop, Dakota stepped back out to the front of the café. "So, Sam, I guess I owe you an apology. Look, I'm sorry, but I must locate George. Do you have any idea where he might be?"

"I'm sorry, sir. As I said before, I don't. I haven't heard from him since he left here early this morning."

Reaching for the door, Dakota glanced back. "Okay then, if you hear from him, would you please ask him to call Allie or me?"

"Wait, Allie?"

"Yes, Allie is the other mutual friend that is trying to locate him."

"Well, I don't know where George is now, but I do know that this morning before he left, he was talking on the phone with someone about a woman named Allie Callahan. He sounded a little concerned and mentioned something about her staying at his farmhouse. That is all I heard because he went back into the kitchen to finish the conversation. A few minutes later, he came out to tell me he was leaving for the day."

"Thank you, Sam. That might help."

Dakota got back into his car and headed up to the farmhouse in Acton. As he drove up to the back, the lights in the kitchen were on. He got out of the car, rushed over to the house, and began ringing the bell that hung just outside the door. In less than a minute, the back door swung open, and another stranger was standing in the doorway. Dakota was shocked to find someone else he didn't know. "Who the hell are you?"

"I could ask you the same question! Who the hell are you? Why are you here at this ungodly time of night?"

"My name is Dakota, and I'm looking for George."

"Well, why didn't you say that in the first place? Come on in."

Dakota stepped into the kitchen to find George sitting at the table. "What the hell is going on, George? Allie has been trying to reach you all day, and you haven't answered any of her calls!"

"Come in, Dakota, and have a seat. I have been rather busy today. Let me introduce you two. Dakota, this is Delsin Hill. Delsin, this is Dakota Channing."

A look of extreme shock came over Dakota's face as he turned, walked up to Delsin, and peered straight into his eyes. "You're Delsin Hill? The same Delsin Hill that was in jail with Makya?"

"I am the very same Delsin, yes, sir."

Dakota turned to George. "What the hell is this guy doing here?"

George went over to the sink to fill the coffeepot. "Please, Dakota, have a seat. I'll make us some coffee. This is going to be a very long night. Delsin and I have a lot to explain to you to get you caught up."

Dakota turned to George. "Why haven't you been returning Allie's phone calls? Did you know that there has been a shooting? Did you know Jake was shot?"

George turned on his heels. "What? Isn't he on his honeymoon?"

"Allie has been trying to reach you to let you know about the shooting and warn you to be careful. They believe Makya was the shooter. She is worried that the reason she can't reach you is that he has somehow gotten to you as well."

Delsin retrieved the coffee filters and coffee from the cabinet. "George, they're probably right...well, partly right."

Dakota was growing more confused as the conversation went on. "What am I missing here? First, what do you mean by 'partly right'?"

George pulled out a chair at the table. "Here, Dakota, sit down. As I told you before, we need to bring you up to speed."

Delsin took a chair at the table. "Look, I believe Makya was involved in the shooting, but I don't think he's the one that actually took the shot. The other thing you should know is that his brother was a sniper in the Army Special Forces. Last I knew, he had a severe case of PTSD and was having a significant issue integrating back into civilian life. I don't think it would be much of a stretch to think that somehow Makya got his brother involved by feeding him some sort of false conspiracy story."

Putting the cream, sugar, and mugs of coffee on the table, George took a seat. "Look, Dakota, Delsin first got in touch with me over a month ago. He's been staying at one of our safe houses for a couple of weeks."

"Are you kidding me? Does Payne know he is here?"

"Yes, but he hasn't told Allie yet. He is going to be part of a new task force to reexamine Allie's case. I believe Payne has asked her to work as a consultant at the station, but originally didn't want her involved with this group. He called me earlier today and told me he was reconsidering that. Maybe we should call Allie right now and let her know I am fine, but I wouldn't mention anything else to her until we have a chance to talk to Payne."

Chapter 15

I was just dozing off again when my cell phone rang.

"Hey, Dakota, did you find George?"

"Yes, he's fine. He has been at the farmhouse all day."

"Thank you so much! Did you tell him about the shooting?"

"Yes. Look, Allie, I'm having coffee with him now, and then I'm heading to Conway."

"No, Dakota, you don't have to do that; we're fine here. Claudia is being discharged in the morning. My mom and Claudia's father, Bill, are here, and they'll give us a ride back to Stanford. Jake is still unconscious, but stable and they plan to transport him to Southern Maine Med tomorrow by noon."

"Are you sure? I don't mind driving out there at all. What about your box? I was going to bring it to you tonight."

"I'm sure. Just get some rest. Do you think you could bring it by the station tomorrow afternoon, though?"

"Sure, I'd be happy to."

"That would be perfect. I'll be there by then. I don't know who will be involved, but Payne is putting a new team together to work on my case. It's my understanding that he has some new people with fresh eyes that will be involved. He has also decided to let me work with them, and I believe it's Payne's intention to get us up and running tomorrow."

The following morning, Mom, Bill, and I went down to the cafeteria for coffee and something to eat. When we got back to Claudia's room, the doctor was there to discharge her.

With some hesitation, he asked, "Would you like to go down to see Jake before we send you on your way?"

"Oh, my God, yes!"

"Okay then, but remember, Claudia, he is still unconscious. I want you to prepare yourself because his head is still bandaged, but not as much as yesterday. What you can see of his face is pretty badly bruised."

"I'm just grateful he is alive. Can I be with him at Southern Maine?"

"Of course! He will be in ICU there, and you will have to follow their protocol, but you are his wife."

"Yes, I am, aren't I? I am so grateful for that."

Claudia turned to me. "He is going to come out of this, right?"

As painful as it was, I had to be honest with her. "Claudia, I don't know."

"You don't have any idea? You have no feeling about Jake?"

Looking rather perplexed, the doctor interjected. "Claudia, no one has a crystal ball. We'll just have to wait and see if Jake's body can fight its way out of this."

I shot Claudia a look, nodding slightly. "That's right, Claudia, no one can truly know what will happen. We just have to be here for Jake and be patient."

The doctor got us a wheelchair for her and directed us to Jake's room. As I pushed her down the hall, Claudia apologized. "I'm so sorry, Allie. I guess I almost outed you to the doctor."

"It's okay; I don't blame you. If the situation were reversed, I'd be asking you the same thing. I just want to keep this whole thing with my intuition under wraps."

When I wheeled Claudia into Jake's room, it was chilling. Seeing him hooked up to machines, IVs, and tubes coming from him unnerved me.

Claudia got up out of the wheelchair and moved over to the bed. She pressed her fingers to her lips and then gently to his. "Jake, I'm here. You're going to be fine. Please, you just have to be. I love you so much, and we have so many memories to still make. We have to finish our honeymoon. You aren't going to cheat me out of that, are you? What about inviting our friends to the Christmas Tree Farm in ten years so we can renew our vows? Remember, we had a deal!"

Resting my hand on her shoulder, I gently squeezed. "Claudia, it's time to go. Our parents are going to be waiting at the hospital entrance for us."

"I know, but—"

"Come on, we should let him rest."

"I know, but I am so scared to leave him. I don't want him to slip away."

"He's fighting hard, Claudia. He is stronger than you think. The sooner we get on our way, the sooner we can get you to Southern Maine Medical. That way, you can be there when he arrives."

"You're right, we do need to get going." Claudia leaned over and kissed him on the forehead. "See you soon, Jake."

A few hours later, I was back at the Stanford police station. I approached the front desk. "Hello, it's Stacy, Stacy Anderson, right?"

"Yes, good memory. Payne is expecting you this afternoon, and he is up in the war room with a few others. He said to send you right up."

"Thank you."

I headed up the stairs, got to the conference room door, and collected my thoughts before entering. So, this was it; I was officially on the Stanford PD payroll. I would now assist in taking down my stalker and help to figure out what happened to Josh. I took a deep breath and stepped into the war room. To my surprise, documents and photographs from my case still covered the whiteboards. They had taken nothing down.

Payne made his way to the door. "Hey, Allie, come on in. The rest of the team is here. I think you know most of them. You remember Detective Hayln Deere from Colorado and Detective Carl Johnson from New York, right?"

"Yes, of course. It's good to see you both again."

When I reached out to shake Hayln's hand, she stepped forward and hugged me. "I can't tell you how glad we are to see you, Allie. We have been so worried."

Payne continued. "And, of course, you know Brian Davis from forensics."

"Hi Brian, good to see you again."

I turned to the last person in the room. "I don't think we've met, have we?"

"Ah, no, I'm sure we haven't."

Payne stood in front of me. "Allie, this is Delsin Hill."

Stunned, I stepped back. "Delsin Hill? Delsin Hill! *Thee* Delsin Hill?"

Delsin raised his hand and gestured to me with apprehension. "Hello, Allie."

"Oh, my God, Payne! What is he doing here?"

"I'm so sorry we're meeting under these circumstances, but yes, I am that same Delsin Hill."

Stepping closer to him, I shrugged. "I don't mean to be rude, but you are the last person I would have expected to be part of this team."

"I'm sure, but when Payne called me and told me about what was going on here, I knew I had to help."

I stepped over to Payne. "Does Dakota and George know he is here?"

Payne reached up, rubbing his forehead. "Yes?"

"Are you telling me or asking me, Payne?"

"Telling you. I need you to remain open-minded long enough to just hear us out."

I was growing angrier by the minute. "I thought this guy is the one that told Makya all about me. How can you trust him?" Turning back to Delsin, I stared him down. "Are you kidding me, Payne?"

I no sooner got the words out when George walked in the door. "Well, it looks like I didn't get here any too soon."

I spun around to face him. "You knew about this? You knew about this and didn't say anything to me?"

"Okay, Allie, I guess I deserve that, but you need to give us time to explain everything to you before you draw any conclusions."

I stopped, closed my eyes, and took a deep breath. I felt a warmth come over me, and in my mind, I could hear, *Listen with your heart, my dear,* and then, there it was, that total calmness that washed over me when I listened with my intuition.

Payne directed the group. "Could I ask you all to take a seat at the conference table? I would like to spend the afternoon putting a strategy together. I don't know about the rest of you, but I've about had it with this Makya!"

I sat down right next to George and addressed him under my breath. "How long have you known about this Delsin thing?"

"About a month."

"About a month? Are you kidding me? Since before Claudia's wedding?"

"Allie, don't forget, you've been missing. I couldn't have told you about Delsin, even if I wanted to. I certainly was not going to bring it up at Claudia's wedding."

Payne ceased our volley. "Could we have just one conversation around this table?"

Pausing, I sat back in my chair. "Sorry, Payne."

"Thank you. First, I would like to give you an update on Detective Carpenter. I just got a call, and he has been transported to Southern Maine. He's there in ICU and is still unconscious but stable. They told me they would notify us if there were any changes.

"Second, Dakota will be part of this team, but is unable to be here this afternoon. Allie, he said he will bring the box with him tomorrow, but if you need it sooner, he wants you to call him.

"And third, I want to address the big gray elephant in the room. I don't think we will get anything accomplished if I don't. Allie, Delsin is here voluntarily. Initially, I contacted him to see if he could give us some insight into what Makya's frame of mind was when he was in prison. Actually, I think I would like him to speak on his own behalf. Delsin, would you mind sharing what you told me with the group?"

"Sure, as Payne said, I spent a year in prison with Makya. While I was inside, he befriended me, using our Native American ties to gain my confidence. Makya told me that his father was a medicine man and an influential member of his tribe. Of course, that wasn't entirely true, but he was able to gain my confidence for that reason. As time went on, we shared more and more about our families, but for some reason, I never quite trusted him enough to talk about exactly what tribe I was from. Once he learned about the elders' disagreement over the ancestral box, he started to show his true colors. When I refused to give him you or your grandfather's names, he grew increasingly volatile. I was relieved that I was released when I was. I couldn't get away from him fast enough. I made certain that when I left prison, I didn't tell any of the inmates where I was headed. Believe me, I wanted to put that whole experience behind me. Saying I had no idea how powerful and gifted he was is an understatement, and I certainly didn't know he had such a thirst for power."

Silence hovered over the room, and it took me a minute to absorb and try to process what I'd just heard. "Let me get this straight. You were incarcerated with this guy, became his friend, gave him your life's story, and then decided you didn't trust him?"

"When you put it that way, it sounds terrible, but yes, that about sums it up."

There were no comments from anyone in the room. They were just sitting there, waiting for me to respond.

Without saying a word, I got up and walked over to the whiteboard. I ran my hand over the document that bore Delsin's name. I looked back at him. "I can live with that, at least for now. I have other questions, but my instincts are blaring at me to accept your word."

Payne glanced around the room with relief on his face and got up from the conference table. Joining me at the whiteboard, he turned. "So, everyone, everything you see on these walls demonstrates the movements and activities of Makya that we are aware of. Since he has shown up here in Stanford, he has already left a few casualties in his wake.

"First, he attacked Allie, who miraculously escaped by plummeting through her office window. Then, on New Year's Eve, Allie's fiancé went missing from his apartment, which was found in total disarray. The most recent casualty is our very own Detective Jake Carpenter, who is now in a coma at Southern Maine Medical."

Chapter 16

Payne wrapped up the meeting with the new task team at about five o'clock but requested a few of us to stay for a bit. After everyone had left the room, except Officer Moretti and Brian Davis from forensic, and me, Payne motioned us to follow him.

Showing us back to his office, he stopped and asked us to wait in the hall. He came back out with a manila folder in his hands. "Okay, you guys, I know you thought your day was done, but I need you for something else this evening." He turned and stepped toward me. "Are you in? You are officially on the payroll now."

"Of course, I'm all in. Duty calls!"

Tapping the folder on the side of his head, he rolled his eyes. "I think our future is showing me that some of us are going to have a long night."

The humor wasn't lost on me as he placed it in my hands. "Would you like me to give that a try?" Mimicking him, I followed suit, tapping my head, and laughed. "Nope, nothing!"

Payne started down the hall, motioning us to follow him. "We're all going to have to keep that sense of humor this evening because I believe this night is going to require it, along with a lot of coffee or whatever your preference is for caffeine intake! I received a text about an hour ago. We need to go down to the morgue. Brian, we have another case, and I will need you to start the autopsy this evening. Let's head down; I'll fill everyone in when we get there."

We took the elevator to the basement and headed down a long hall to a door on the far end. The police station was an old brick building and painted concrete blocks made up the cellar hallway.

A chill shot through me. "This certainly fits all the typical stereotypes for the location of a morgue! Why are they always in the basement? It's kind of creepy."

No one responded, and Brian opened the door. "Come on in."

Entering the room, the bright and finished office, clad with a large oak desk and matching bookshelves, took me by surprise. In the corner was a small refrigerator and a coffee bar with cabinets above. It was not at all what I expected after coming down that dark and dreary hallway we took to get there. It was quite pleasant, bright, and cheery. On the far side of the office was another door, and a shaded window to see into the adjoining room.

"Wow, this is not at all what I expected. I thought we would walk into a sterile, clinical room that smelled like, like—I don't know what, but definitely not like this."

Walking to the window, I brushed my hand over the oak casing around it and then turned. "This is not at all what I expected."

Brian showed us over to a closet. "You can hang your coats in here. I'm sure this isn't how most people envision a morgue, but I can assure you, it is." He pointed across the room. "I believe the room on the other side of that window and door is what you would have expected."

Payne interrupted. "Allie, in that folder is a picture. Before you open it, I want you to be prepared. Also, I want to make sure you are ready to be here and help us in this way. A morgue is not the first place I would have taken you to get your work started, but unfortunately, sometimes it's just part of the job."

"I think I'll be fine, Payne, but we'll see, won't we?"

After opening the folder, I looked up. "Wow!"

Stepping away from the others, I studied the photo. It was a rather washed-out, faxed photocopy of a young woman, probably in her late teens or early twenties. Her face was pale and chalky, and her neck was slit from ear to ear. I was entirely unprepared for what I was looking at, but not in the way Payne thought. As I traced my hand over the photo, a looming sense of anger and confusion swept over me. "This poor girl, she can't be much more than nineteen or twenty."

Brian opened the door that led to the backroom, exposing that strange, sterile smell I had expected. When we stepped into the room, it was full of easy-to-clean stainless-steel surfaces. Much to my surprise, that room was even more extensive than the first. On the far left wall was a deep stainless-steel sink with a bank of metal drawers on each side. Lined up in front of the sink and drawers were four metal tables, each draped with a white sheet. To the right of those tables was a bank of refrigerated drawers with stainless-steel fronts. There was a wide double door in the back of the room, and on the last wall , there was rolling metal shelving stocked with supplies and boxes.

Brian smiled. "This is what you expected, right?"

I scanned the room. "Yes, exactly."

There was a knock at the double door in the back of the room. When Brian opened it, I smelled car exhaust. It was a garage, and there were two men with a gurney on the other side of the doors.

"Good evening. Here she is."

Brian stepped aside. "Hi, Ed, you got the late shift with Jerry?"

As they rolled the gurney in and up next to one of the stainless-steel tables, Jerry laughed. "I'm stuck with this guy for a whole month."

Brian walked to one drawer and pulled a triangular-shaped block out as Payne and Antonio stepped up to one side of the table and carefully helped the two EMTs move her over from the gurney. He handed it to Payne. "Could you place this under her neck?"

Ed reached out with a plastic bag and a manila envelope. "Here, Payne, this is her personal effects and the paperwork from the hospital."

As I stood there, it struck me that this was just routine for these guys. I mean, they just wheeled in a young woman who was barely cold, and it was just a matter of business. I guess they had to handle things that way when doing this type of work, but it was just another day at the office for these guys.

As Ed and Jerry left the room, I stepped up to the table. Still covered by a cotton blanket, I saw the small, shapely outline of her body. This was someone's daughter, maybe someone's sister, and someone's friend, but I knew I needed to find a way to separate myself from that as well.

Payne interrupted my thoughts. "Allie, are you okay?"

"Yeah, amazingly enough, I am. I wasn't sure how I was going to feel, but I'm okay."

We all stood around the table.

That feeling of confusion and anger came over me again, and as I looked across the table, I saw the young girl standing next to Payne. Looking directly at Payne, I didn't acknowledge her as she spoke. "What am I doing here? What the hell are they doing?"

Brian grabbed the top of the cover over her head and looked directly at me. "You ready?"

"Ready."

Carefully, he pulled the cover down to her shoulders. "She lost a tremendous amount of blood. The assailant hit the jugulars on both sides of her neck."

That wave of confusion and anger escalated as I glanced up, and she was still there. "What? What is that? Am I dreaming? What is going on?"

I hesitated, trying to ignore her. "That's a clean-cut, isn't it?"

The young woman appeared between Brian and me. "You can see me. I know you can. I could see it when you glanced up. Why don't they see me? Stop ignoring me!"

Moving over to him, I shook my head. "Excuse me, Brian, I'm sorry, I was distracted. Can you repeat that?"

"No problem. It looks like this cut was made with a surgical instrument by someone who knew what they were doing. As I said, this guy got both jugulars, but they did it with one clean swipe of the blade. If I didn't know better, I would say that when it was done, this girl had to be out cold because if she wasn't, any struggle would not have allowed such a remarkable cut."

The young girl was silent. I would have expected her to respond to that comment, and when I turned, she was not there.

Payne reached out and tapped Antonio on the shoulder. "I don't think there is much more we can do here until Brian gets through this autopsy tonight. I'm going to stay here with him, but there is no reason for us all to be here. Allie's car is here in the parking lot, and I know she wants to go by and check in with Claudia at the hospital. Why don't you follow her to Southern Maine Med and then to the Summit?"

Payne turned to address me. "You're staying with your mom at the Summit, for now, right?"

"Yes, I am. If Antonio doesn't mind, I would love to see Claudia and Jake."

Payne reached out and took my hand. "It's settled then. Antonio will need to stay with you until further notice."

Chapter 17

A ntonio walked me to the car. "Hey, Allie, nice ride!"
"I know, but it's not mine. It's Dakota's car. My mom put mine in storage when I was at George's."

"You mean when you went missing?"

"Well, yes, technically speaking, but from my point of reference, I was at George's for the weekend." I know sooner spoke when I had a flash of memory. I remembered sitting in the woods warmed by a fire, wrapped in the safety of a matronly woman's arms. It was a flash, and then it disappeared.

"Allie? Hey, Allie, are you all right?"

I nodded. "I'm fine. Let's get this caravan going. Where is your car?"

He pointed to the next row. "It's right there. Let me warm it up for a second, and I'll swing around so I can get behind you, and we can head out."

"Okay."

I got in the car, started it up, and looked in the rear view mirror. The young woman from the morgue was sitting in my back seat. Seeing her was startling, but once again, I ignored her. She wasn't having it.

"You can pretend you don't see or hear me, but until you acknowledge me, I am sticking to you like glue. After all, I need to help you figure out what happened to me because I guess—" She cleared her throat. "Well, I guess I'm dead?"

We headed over to the hospital, and when Antonio and I entered ICU, Claudia was coming out of Jake's room. She rushed over and wrapped her arms around me.

"OMG, girl! I am so glad to see you. I was just heading down to the cafeteria to get something lite to eat. Will you come with?"

"Of course, I think I could eat something myself. Any change with Jake?"

"No, he is stable. They did some tests, and the good news is there is brain function. They keep saying that it's all up to him now. He needs to fight to come back to us."

We got a bite to eat and then headed back to Jake's room. They only allowed two visitors in the room at a time, so Antonio stationed himself outside the door and gave the officer there a break.

Claudia and I stood on opposite sides of Jake's bed. "He's a strong bugger, Allie. I know he'll get back to me. We have so much more life to live."

Closing my eyes, I could hear Jake's voice. "Allie, tell Claudia, I'm just resting my body. I'll be back to her soon."

Shocked, I opened my eyes. There he was, plain as day, standing next to her.

"You can see me, right?"

"Ah, yes, but—"

"I know, crazy, right?"

Claudia reached over and waved her hand in my face. "Allie, what is it?"

"You are not going to believe this!"

"Try me, I bet I will!"

"Jake is standing right next to you."

"What? You're kidding, right? Oh, my God, he's not dead, is he?"

"No, Claudia, look at the monitors. His heart is beating, and he is stable!"

"What then?"

"He said to tell you he is just resting and he will not leave you. He'll be back with you shortly."

"What? You can actually see him? I mean, that's crazy!"

I smiled. "That's exactly what he said."

I blinked. He was still there. "Allie, I need to talk to you about Josh. I saw him!"

"Oh, my God, what do you mean you saw him?"

Claudia's eyes widened. "Allie, what's going on? What is he saying?"

I raised my hand to silence her. "Wait, Claudia."

Tears welled in my eyes as I feared the worst. "Jake—"

"No, Allie, he was here, he's alive." With that, Jake disappeared.

"Allie, what the hell?"

"He's gone, but Jake said that Josh was here and he's alive, and then he was gone."

Claudia stepped around the bed and put her arm around me. "What the hell, Allie! What is happening to you?

Suddenly, the young girl was standing directly in front of us. "Okay, if you could see him, I know you can see me."

Breaking from Claudia's grasp, I dropped my arms to my sides. "Okay, I can see you, but I don't know what you want from me?"

Claudia grabbed my hands. "Is it, Jake? Is he back?"

Shaking her loose for a second time, I spun around. "Can everyone just stop for a minute?"

The room went silent.

"I'm sorry, Claudia. I know you are the only one here, well, at least physically, but in reality, we aren't alone. There is a young girl here that has followed me from the morgue."

"What? What are you talking about, Allie? I think you have to get a grip!"

The young girl backed off. "I'm sorry. This is all so confusing to me. I just don't understand any of it. There has to be a good reason that you can see me, right?"

I began pacing the floor as I addressed Claudia. "I can explain, but first, just give me a minute."

I looked straight at the young woman. "Okay, all right, I'm sorry, too. I can sense your anger and confusion. In fact, I felt that before I could even see you. What's your name?"

"My name is Alexandra Stevens, but people call me Alex. Well, they did call me Alex, I mean when I was alive."

"Okay, Alex, if you want help, you have got to give me some space. You also need to realize that if I talk to you around other people, they will have me committed. This is my friend, Claudia. She is safe. She knows me and will understand when I explain all this to her, but talking around anyone else is off-limits unless I tell you otherwise. Deal?"

"Deal!"

Claudia seemed frazzled. "Can someone, and I do mean you, Allie, fill me in on this whole conversation because, as you well know, I can only hear half of it?"

I sat down in the visitor's chair and cradled my head in my hands. "I am having some difficulty keeping up with everyone. Believe me, Claudia, sometimes the room is a lot more crowded than you think."

I stood. "Okay, I need both of you to just let me talk. Claudia, I am working on a new case with Payne, which involves this young woman. Her name is Alex. This evening before I came here, Payne, Antonio, Brian from forensics, and I went to the morgue to get started on her case. While we were there, EMTs transported her body into the morgue. I suspect that when Brian pulled the cover off her face, it was a shock to Alex because it was her laying there. Based on her reaction, I'm quite sure that until then, she didn't even know she was dead."

Alex threw up her hands. "That's the understatement!"

117

Turning to her, I shot her a piercing look. She raised her hands in surrender. "Okay, okay, I'll stop."

Claudia chuckled, shaking her head. "I don't know what she just said, but it looks like our new friend, Alex, has a hard time containing herself as well."

Pausing, I raised my hands. "Are you both going to listen?" Giving them another chance to remain silent, I went on. "Okay then, where was I? Oh yes, well, when we were in the morgue, try as I might to ignore Alex, she persisted and followed me here. That about brings you up to speed because you both know what has transpired since I got here.

"Look, Alex, as far as I know, I am the only one that can see or hear you, so you will have to remember that if you're going to be hanging around."

"All right, all right, I get it."

I turned to Claudia. "Alex says she understands, but I guess that is yet to be seen. Can we get back to our conversation about Josh? What do you think? How do you think Jake was able to see him?"

Moving back over next to Jake's bed, Claudia looked down at him. "Well, if he is floating around outside of his body, maybe he did see him." She shrugged, skeptically. "He could have possibly seen Josh here in another part of the hospital, but why wouldn't Josh just come to see us? Allie, something is off. Do you think maybe Josh has passed and Jake didn't realize it?"

"I hope not. I hope Jake did see him alive, and there is some good explanation as to why he hasn't got in touch with us. That's always possible."

Chapter 18

It was nine-thirty when I headed over to my mother's. Antonio walked me to my car so he could follow me home. When I got behind the wheel, I looked in the rear view mirror, and much to my relief, Alex wasn't there.

When I pulled up to the entrance of the Summit, Henry opened my door. "Are you in for the evening, Allie?"

"Yes, thank you. It's been a very long couple of days, and I need a good night's sleep."

Antonio had gotten out of his car behind me. "Good evening, Henry. I'll be staying here tonight."

As we made our way through the lobby, Antonio paused at the desk. "Sandy, I'll be posted at the entrance of the penthouse for the night. You have my cell number, so please don't hesitate to call me if you need something or if anything seems at all suspicious."

"Yes, I certainly will."

We took the elevator to the penthouse, and when we stepped out, I couldn't help notice the large clock in the hallway read ten-fifteen. "Antonio, I'm going to take a shower and head off to bed. It looks like Mom and Guile have turned in already. Why don't you pull the recliner from the great room out here so you can at least be comfortable this evening?"

I don't think that will be necessary. I'll just sit in the high-back chair near the elevator. I don't want to get too comfortable."

"Well, I'm sure I'll sleep much better knowing you're here. Thank you so much for everything. I'll see you in the morning."

"Goodnight, Allie. You know where I'll be if you need me."

After making my way to my room, I grabbed my robe and slippers, and headed to the shower. Standing in front of the bathroom vanity, I stared into the mirror. "Josh, where are you? With all of my gifts, I can't feel you or get a sense if you are even still with us." Closing my eyes, I thought, *I just don't get it.*

I nearly jumped out of my skin when I heard a voice.

"If it's any consolation, I don't think I have seen anyone hanging around you named Josh."

Startled, I opened my eyes to find Alex standing to my right. "Geeze, Alex, you scared me. You just can't keep popping up anywhere you want."

"Sorry, but sometimes when you need an answer, I seem to find myself in your presence. Like I said, I see plenty of people around you, but I haven't heard the name Josh."

"I'm not sure if that makes me feel better or gives me the creeps. It's kind of unnerving knowing there are others following me around during my private moments."

"It's not like that, Allie. I can't explain it, but it's just not."

"Well, if it's not, then get out of here. Scoot. Vamoose. Leave so I can take a shower in private and stop popping up and startling me!"

I stepped into the shower and soaked myself from head to toe, brushing my fingers through my hair. It felt amazing, and as my body grew accustomed to the temperature, I continued adjusting the heat, making it hotter and hotter. As I let the hot water pour down over me, my nerves just seemed to melt away. Placing my hands on the shower wall to brace myself, I allowed the hot water to flow down over my lower back, melting away more of the day's tension.

The shower had served its purpose, and I now felt physically and emotionally spent. I stepped out, dried off, and slid on my robe. I couldn't wait another minute to climb into bed. As I was drifting off, I couldn't stop thinking about Alex. She seemed to be a nice enough young woman, and I was even able to find a little humor in the fact that she was so determined to get my attention. I knew I would certainly need to come up with some sort of ground rules for her. What that would look like, I wasn't sure.

Mercifully, I fell into a deep slumber and slept through the entire night, until, of course, I smelled the aroma of fresh-baked muffins wafting from the oven. Mom was at it again.

I got up, slid on some jeans and a sweatshirt, and headed to the kitchen. Hearing me coming, she had already poured me a coffee. "Coffee with cream only, my dear, just the way you like it!"

"Oh, just what I need. Thank you so much, Mom. I do love waking up here in the morning to the smell of your fresh-baked muffins."

"Thanks, Al. I think Guile does, too."

"Mom, I think I'll take Antonio something to eat. I know he won't leave his post at the door."

I'm one step ahead of you. I already took him some. I know Guile must smell the muffins, and I expect him to appear any minute. By the way, I was wondering what your plans were for today."

"Why, did you have something you needed me for?"

"No, I was just thinking we need to get your car out of storage soon and go to the dealership if you're still thinking about trading it in."

"I am, but this morning I'm heading over to the police station. Payne has me working with them on a new case."

"Really? I thought he was putting you on the task team regarding Makya."

They have, but this has become my priority, at least for now. Last night they brought a young woman in who was found murdered. I don't know the details yet, but I'm sure I will learn more today."

I thought for a minute, then realized I was rambling. "Mom, I have an important question for you. I'm not sure if it's anything you can help me with, but I just don't know who to turn to. If Grandfather were here, I would ask him, but he's not."

She reached out and steadied me with her hand. "Allie, just spill it!"

Do you think Grandfather was able to communicate at all with those who have passed? I mean, people who have, ah—you know, people who have died?"

"Your grandfather had many gifts. As for that one, I'm not sure. But you know what? I remember your dad talked about his mother having the ability to see things he referred to as beyond the veil, whatever that means."

"So, Gram was gifted as well? I mean, I know she was into the healing arts using homeopathic and herbal methods, but I didn't know she was gifted in other ways."

Suddenly I had a flash of a memory. "Mom, remember I told you I had fallen asleep at George's, reading that book you found?"

"How could I forget?"

"Well, I think I'm slowly remembering things. I thought I fell asleep, and that I dreamed about meeting an older woman in the woods, but Mom, I was missing for six months. Where the hell was I all that time? Maybe I got hurt and wandered off somewhere and had amnesia or something?"

Guile walked in. "Sorry to interrupt. I wasn't eavesdropping, but I overheard you talking, and there are a couple of major problems with your amnesia theory, Allie."

Mom handed Guile a coffee. "And what would that be?"

"First off, Christina, when you and Claudia went to look for Allie, you found all her things just laying around like she just vanished into thin air. There were no signs of a struggle or anything to suggest foul play. Even Payne said that, and more importantly, Allie, after your so-called dream, you woke up right where you thought you fell asleep. In the exact same spot."

Lifting my coffee, taking a small sip, I took a deep breath and blew out a puff of air. "That is true."

Mom placed the muffins in the center of the table. "Allie, he does have a point."

Grabbing a muffin from the plate, and in frustration, I rolled my eyes. "Everything is coming back to me in bits and pieces. I vaguely remember seeing that young girl in the hospital gown, who finally spoke and told me that she was actually me, from my youth."

As I was speaking more memories started to unfold. "Wait, that's right, there was a horse. I rode him into the woods where I came across that woman. I'm not clear yet how long it took me to get to her. I can still feel the sting of the air that was growing increasingly damp and cool. That's right, she invited me to sit by a fire and wrapped us both up in what I think was a bearskin blanket. She seemed strangely familiar, and although I couldn't hear her voice, she spoke to me, and I could listen to her words in my head. More importantly, she referred to me as the daughter of her daughter's son.

Wouldn't that make her my great-grandmother on Dad's side of the family? I mean, wouldn't that have made her dad's grandmother?"

Hesitating, Mom got up from the table and began pacing the floor. "This just keeps getting stranger and stranger. Allie, that means the woman you met in the woods was Catori. Remember what I told you about her?"

"I do. You said that she was the only woman that has ever had the honor of being the holder of the ancestral box."

My cell phone rang, interrupting our conversation. It was Payne. Motioning to my mother for a break in the conversation, I answered the phone. "Good morning, Payne."

"Good morning, Allie. Are you coming to the station this morning?"

"I sure am. I should be there in about an hour."

"Great, see you then."

"That's my cue. I'm being summoned to my new job. I don't mean to be rude, but I've got to finish eating and get on the road."

Guile stood, leaned over, and gently kissed my mother on the cheek. "Well, I'm heading down to the lobby to work. I'll see you two later."

I stood. "Got to go, Mom. Don't wait for me for supper. Depending on how the day goes, it could be a late night."

She stopped me before I could get out the door. "Allie, somehow I feel like we got off topic during our whole breakfast conversation."

Throwing my bag over my shoulder, I picked up my keys. "What?"

"What were all those questions about seeing dead people?"

I chuckled. "Oh, that! Yes, it would seem that is just another one of my many gifts. I can see dead people."

"Wait, what?"

"I know, it's a shocker. Right?"

"Allie, you just can't drop a bomb like that and leave me hanging here!"

"I know, I'm sorry, Mom, but I have to get to the station. Look, just to put your mind to ease, it's nothing scary or creepy, and it isn't just dead people. You know Jake is in a coma, right?"

"Yes."

"Well, how should I put this? Last night, when I was at the hospital visiting, I saw him standing next to Claudia, outside his body. It's like some people have moved to a different dimension or some other level of consciousness. They just pop up out of the blue, and I can see them when no one else can. Although it seems they appear to me when they are looking for help, I am noticing that they also show up on the scene to help me when I need something. I haven't quite figured it all out yet. Things seem to be unfolding slowly. Sometimes, I can't make rhyme or reason out of the gifts I have been given, but I guess that just comes with the territory for now."

Chapter 19

Within the hour, Officer Antonio Moretti dropped me off at the police station. The minute I walked through the door, Sandy at the front desk raised her hand to signal me. "Good morning, Allie. Payne has been waiting for you and told me to send you directly to his office."

"Hi, Sandy, thanks. I'll head right up there."

I stepped into Payne's empty office. Taking a chair across from his desk, I heard his voice. "Don't get too comfortable. We're going down to Brian's office."

"You mean the morgue?"

"Yes, but it sounds better when I say his office. I have been part of the force for thirty-five years, but being in the morgue still gives me the creeps. If I haven't gotten used to it by now, I'm sure I never will!"

Payne's phone rang. "Hello, Payne here." The look on his face turned sour as he listened to the voice on the other end. "Well, well, long time since we've heard from you." He stopped to listen again before responding. "What makes you think I would ever give you that satisfaction? What's the problem? Has there been another little interruption in your plans? What a shame!"

Slamming down the phone, he sat hard in his chair. "That son of a bitch! That arrogant asshole! He's got a lot of gall."

"Payne, was that Makya?"

"It sure as hell was! He hung up on me, but I can tell you this much, he is even angrier than I am."

"I don't know about that, Payne. I've never seen you lose it like that before."

"Well, stick around, 'cause this guy is really testing my patience. I can't wait to get my hands on him, lock him up, and throw away the damn key."

"What the hell did he say?"

"I can't repeat exactly what he said, but basically, he said we were effing lucky that Jake survived. He'll make sure that doesn't happen again. Then when I responded to him, he called me a few more choice words before he hung up."

Dakota walked into Payne's office. "What's all the commotion about? I could hear you all the way down the hall."

"Payne just received an irate call from Makya, saying that Jake was lucky to have survived. If you ask me, I think he was on a fishing expedition."

"Why do you say that? It sounds to me like he's just escalating again. That's his MO, isn't it?"

"I think he is, but he can't know for sure about Jake's status or condition because there hasn't been anything on the news about Jake since the shooting. In fact, there wasn't much coverage on it even the day it happened. Right, Payne?"

"Yes, we're trying to keep the status on the whole case, including Jake's condition, out of the media for now. You're probably right, Allie, but that creep still gets under my skin."

Dakota set my wooden box on Payne's desk. "Here you go, Allie. I'm sorry I didn't get it here yesterday." He glanced at Payne. "I'll be down in the war room with Delsin, Tanis, George, and Carl, working with them. Let me know if there is anything else I can help you with."

"Can you fill them in on the call I got from Makya? It might have lasted a mere thirty seconds, but I want them to know he made contact."

"Sure thing."

Stepping over to him, I hugged him. "Thank you, Dakota. I appreciate your bringing this to me. I think I might be needing it today."

As he walked out the door, he called back. "I'm not even going to ask!"

Payne picked up the box. "I'm not asking either. Come on, let's head down to Brian's office or, as you so delicately put it, 'The morgue.'"

Chapter 20

Heading downstairs, we stopped at the front desk. "Stacy, I'll be down in Brian's office if you need me. I have already forwarded my phone."

She smiled at Payne. "The morgue?"

"Yes, dammit, the morgue! Allie and I will be in Brian's office outside the morgue."

I shot her a smile and shrugged.

We found Brian sitting at his desk when we got there.

"Come on in. I'm just making a few more entries on the computer. I have some interesting things to tell you this morning."

The shade to the window of the morgue was up. Payne stood in front of it and stared through at Alex's body. "I really want to get the guy who did this. We need to get a break somewhere!"

Brian got up from his desk and moved to the door leading to the morgue. "Come on in, I have some news for you guys."

Payne picked up the folder. "She's still listed as a Jane Doe, right Brian?"

I moved over to the table. "Her name is Alexandra Stevens."

Looking up, his face was twisted in confusion. "How did you figure that out? We haven't even identified her yet?"

"Ah, no, you didn't, but she did."

Brian shook his head in disbelief. "I definitely want to hear this one! How about you, Payne?"

"I have a feeling I'm not going to like it, but yes, I do want to hear it."

I knew I would have told them, anyway. I may as well rip off the bandage and get it out of the way as soon as possible. "Well, it's like this. When we came down here to the morgue last night, while you were standing next to Alex on the table, I saw her standing next to you. I tried to ignore her, but she did not give up that easily. She followed me for the rest of the evening. First to my car, then the hospital, and finally to my mother's."

Brian looked down at Alex on the table. "Holy shit, Allie. In all my time doing this work, I have never had that kind of experience. That is just insane!"

Stretching his neck from side to side, as he often did when stressed, Payne spun around and went to the door of the office. "I need a coffee. Brian, do you have some out there?"

"I certainly do. I think we could all use one while Allie tells us whatever it is she needs to share."

We stepped out into Brian's office, got a coffee, and sat down at the small round table in the corner. Payne took a sip of his coffee. "All right, Allie, let her rip! I guess there is no time like the present."

I grimaced. "It would seem that I have another talent, and that would be my ability to speak to those that are on…how can I put this…on another plane?"

Brian tipped his head with a slight frown. "You mean you see dead people? I mean, you see their spirit walking around outside their body?"

Turning to Payne to see how he was reacting, I shrugged. "Well yes, but not just dead people."

His eyes grew as big as saucers. "Well, what other people would you be able to see if they weren't, like here, I mean in the flesh? To my knowledge, there are live people, and then there are dead people, right?"

I thought, *Okay, here goes the rest of the bandage.* "I can talk to people who aren't dead yet, but kind of in a state of limbo."

"Limbo?"

"Yeah, like Jake, who is in a coma."

Payne stood from his chair. "Are you saying you communicated with Jake? While he was in a coma, he slipped out of his body to talk to you, but he wasn't dead?"

"Yes, that's exactly what I'm saying. I didn't call you last night about it for two reasons. The first being I really wasn't able to learn anything that could help us. More importantly, I didn't think it was something I should tell you until we were face-to-face."

Brian broke into laughter at my comment, dribbling his coffee down the front of his shirt. "You think?"

"Look, you two, the only thing Jake was concerned about was Claudia. He asked me to tell her he was just resting and he would be back with her shortly, whatever that means! As for Alex, she and I had a couple of conversations, but she didn't even know she was dead until she saw her body laying here in the morgue, much less remember what happened that put her there! I'm sure this newfound gift of mine will be of use at some point, but not yet. When it is, you'll both be the first to know."

Taking a sip of my coffee, I paused and took a breath. "I think our time would be better spent examining the evidence you uncovered last night, Brian, not chasing these ghosts or whatever you choose to call them."

They both laughed. Payne reached over and tapped Brian on the back. "Man, she sure put us in our place, didn't she? Even more, she's absolutely right!"

I snickered. "I did, didn't I?"

Brian raised his coffee cup. "I can see you will be a valuable asset to our team, Allie. If for nothing else, you will most certainly keep us all in line and focused."

Feeling a little bothered by how I had reacted, I offered an apology. "I don't mean to be short. I'm not frustrated with you, and I'm so grateful to have this opportunity. It's just...it's just that I find this whole gift discovery process so challenging."

Brian quickly took over and changed the course of the conversation. "Hey, like I said, I have some interesting news for you both."

Getting up from the table, he tossed his paper cup in the trash can and went back into the morgue to retrieve Alexandra's case folder. Returning to the table, he slid back into his seat and tilted his head just slightly. "Things aren't always what they seem on the surface, literally!"

Refilling my cup, I squinted. "Literally? I would take that to mean her death wasn't caused by her throat being cut."

"Exactly! The cuts were indeed precise and deep, severing the jugulars on both sides of her neck. The problem with that being the cause of death is that there was still too much blood left in her body, indicating that her heart was not beating when she was cut. Also, it was clear from the scene that she was moved there after her death. Based on the autopsy, I would say her death was roughly twenty-four hours before she was actually found. I sent her stomach contents and blood to the lab. I'm expecting to hear back on those shortly. I called in a favor and put a rush on it. I want to get as much information as I can, as quickly as possible, so we can get this guy before the trail goes cold. Allie's right. Her name is Alexandra Stevens, and her mother is one of our own."

Payne reached over and spun the folder around to him. "One of our own?"

"Yes, her mother is Sara Stevens, a technician at our forensics lab. Not only that, but her father is Arthur Stevens."

"Arthur Stevens? *The* Arthur Stevens, as in Arthur Stevens, the assistant DA?"

"Yes, sir, the very same!"

Chapter 21

After lunch, Payne and I headed upstairs to see how things were going regarding Makya's case. As we entered the war room, my cell phone rang. It was Claudia.

"Hey, Allie!"

I couldn't discern by the excitement in her voice if she was excited or distressed.

"Allie, it's Jake!"

"Claudia, what is it? Is he okay?"

"He is! He really is! Allie, he's been coming around for about an hour! He opened his eyes and actually complained about his head hurting!"

"Oh, my God, that's amazing!"

Payne moved over next to me. "What is it?"

I waved my hand to put him off for a second. "Claudia, I'll let Payne know, and I'll be down to see you both as soon as I get done here at the station."

Payne persisted. "What is going on? Is Jake awake? Can I talk to Claudia?"

I signaled with my hand and mouthed, *Give me one second.* "Claudia, Payne would like to speak with you."

"Sure, of course, put him on."

With a sigh of relief, I handed Payne my cell. "It's great news!"

"Settling into the chair at the conference table, he began fidgeting with his pen. "Claudia, Allie says you have good news?"

"I absolutely do! Jake is awake. The doctors said he is now stable and out of the woods. He says to tell you he has a splitting headache and feels a little under the weather, but besides that, he's back!"

"That's great news, Claudia. Tell him how glad I am that he is on the mend, and I will get over to see him as soon as possible."

"I will for sure. Thank you, Payne, and I'll let you know if there are any more changes."

"Please do that. I'll see you both soon."

Hanging up, he placed both hands on the conference table. Pushing himself from his seat, he turned and handed my phone back to me. "Allie, why don't you go over to the hospital now? There isn't anything we can do here until we get all the forensics back. Go on, get out of here. I'll have Officer Caswell escort you, and Officer Moretti can meet you there at the start of his shift and relieve Caswell then."

By two o'clock, Caswell and I were at the hospital. When I walked into Jake's room, Claudia bounded out of her chair and ran into my arms.

"I'm so glad you're here! Can you believe it?"

Rushing over to Jake's bed, I looked down at him and smirked. "Well, partner, you are like a cat with nine lives. How many is this now? Three?"

He grumbled. "I don't know, I've lost count."

I dropped another hint. "Well then, partner, you will have to be more careful from now on. I guess it will be up to me to keep you safe from here on out."

Blinking to clear his vision and maybe his head, he shot back, "Oh yeah, well, who is going to protect *you*, then?"

"I guess that would be you. Isn't that what partners do for each other?"

Groggy from the pain meds, he managed a whisper, "Yeah, right!" and then he was asleep again.

Claudia looked absolutely exhausted. "Hey, what do you say we go to get something to eat in the cafeteria? It looks like he'll be in and out for a while longer, and you look like you could use a break and a bite to eat!"

"You know what? I actually feel a twinge of hunger coming on. That pang of nausea finally seems to have left me, so you're on!"

On our way to the cafeteria, Claudia stopped at the nurse's station. The nurse sitting at the desk looked up.

"Hi, Mrs. Carpenter, can I help you with something?"

"I just wanted to let someone know that I was going to go down to grab something to eat with my friend, but I will still be here in the hospital if you need me."

Officer Caswell and the officer on duty were both seated outside Jake's room. Although I already knew the answer, I posed the question. "Claudia and I are headed down to get a bite to eat. Do one of you need to go with us, or can we go on our own?"

Caswell scoffed. "You know the rules. I'm coming. Besides, I could use something to eat myself."

Riding on the elevator to go down to the cafeteria, it stopped at the second floor. When the doors opened, no one was there. Looking down the hall directly across from the elevator, we saw someone walking in the opposite direction. The doors were closing as Claudia and I turned to face each other. I could feel my heart pounding. "Was that—?"

Claudia lunged to keep the elevator doors from closing, but it was too late!

"Oh, my God, Claudia, did that look like Josh walking down the hall?"

Stunned, Caswell blurted, "Josh? Josh Sullivan?"

When the elevator doors reopened on the first floor, Claudia and I dashed out and around the corner to the staircase with Caswell on our heels. As we climbed the stairs, he was yelling out to us. "Hey you two, what are you doing?"

When we got back to the second floor, we looked in both directions.

Claudia pointed down the hall. "He was down there. You go that way. I'll try the other hall and meet you back here!"

Five minutes later, we were back at the elevator.

Waiting there for us, Caswell was so angry, he looked like he was going to explode. He shook his head in disbelief. "You can't do that again. How can I keep an eye on both of you if you are going in two different directions?"

With the wind out of my sails, I stood there in a state of shock. "I could have sworn that was Josh. I mean, I know we couldn't see his face, but that guy's build, hair, and gait!"

Claudia rolled her eyes. "Well, one thing is for certain, whoever it was, is very much alive because I saw him, too!"

Blowing a long sigh through my lips, I looked back down the hall. "I'm not sure if that makes me feel any better, but one thing I can say with certainty is that we are both tired and worn out. I think we both need a meal and a good night's sleep. It probably wouldn't hurt you to come home tonight and get some rest after you check back in on Jake."

The elevator door opened again, and Caswell stepped in, holding it open for us.

Claudia ignored him and chuckled. "Yeah, you're right." As she lifted her arm, a look of disdain came over her face. "Pew! One thing is for sure; besides sleep, I definitely need a shower and a change of clothes."

"Well, my friend, I'm glad to see you still have that great sense of humor!."

"Is that what that was? I thought I was just being downright honest."

Caswell grunted. "Hello? I'm over here holding the elevator for you two!"

Joining him in the elevator to head down to eat, we responded in unison. "Sorry!"

Caswell got his meal last and joined us at the table. Sitting across from us, he hesitated to collect his thoughts. "So, would either of you like to explain to me what just happened in the elevator? I get that you responded impulsively because you thought you saw Josh, but you need to realize that you could have put one or both of you in danger by those actions. If something like that happens again, regardless, you need to stop, think and move with a plan. Especially you, Allie. If you're going to be working with Jake, you have got to operate from a different frame of mind."

I looked across at Claudia and then at Caswell. "You're right. I reacted to the emotion of the moment. It was such a shock to see that guy in the hallway. I could have sworn it was Josh. I mean, I realize that isn't likely—" I shifted my gaze to Claudia. "Why would he be back and not contact me?"

She lifted her glass and paused. "That's a great question, but it did look like him, and do I need to remind you about what Jake said?"

Resting his fork on his plate, Caswell looked questioningly. "What? What did Jake say?"

I shot Claudia a warning look, and to recover she stammered out, "He was just rambling when he was coming to." She quickly changed the subject. "What is all this about your working with Jake? Is that what you were trying to tell him when you were talking to him upstairs and you kept referring to him as partner?"

"Yes, when he is better, he and I are going to be working together on the Makya investigation. Not in the field, but the research."

Claudia and I certainly both had our appetites back. Dinner in the cafeteria that evening was meatloaf, mashed potatoes, carrots, and a roll. We devoured everything and then topped it off with a brownie for dessert.

As we finished eating, we got up from the table to take our trays back. "I think my eyes were definitely bigger than my stomach. I should not have eaten so much. Ugh!"

We made our way back upstairs and found Antonio waiting for us outside Jake's room. He was smiling from ear to ear. "Hey, Claudia, I'm so glad Jake has woke up. That's great news!"

Reaching out, wrapping her arms around his neck, she hugged him. "Thanks, Antonio! And thanks for taking such good care of my bestie here. I am so grateful to all of you on the force.

"If you don't mind, I think I am going to catch a ride with you and Allie tonight and go home to get some sleep." She chuckled. "And more importantly, a shower. Let me look in on Jake, speak with the nurse, and I'll be ready to leave.

Chapter 22

Antonio followed Claudia and me back to the Summit. During our ride back, I called my mother to let her know about Jake's improvement and that I would be staying with Claudia for the night.

When we arrived, we entered the foyer, dropped our keys on the table and , Antonio stationed himself just inside the apartment. It occurred to me that it had been six months since I had crossed that threshold. The last time I was there, it was Claudia's and my apartment. Now it was hers with Jake.

Claudia grabbed my hand and led me to her studio. "Al, I have a surprise for you."

In the far corner of the room, a canvas was on her easel draped with a long white sheet that kept it from view.

Leading me over, Claudia positioned me about six feet in front of it. "Close your eyes!"

Amazed, I closed my eyes. "You finished it? This is my house warming present, isn't it?"

"Yes, it is. I wanted it done when you got back. I never gave up on you, Allie! Now keep your eyes closed, no cheating."

Waiting with great anticipation, I heard Claudia slide the sheet off the canvas.

"Okay, ready!"

When I opened my eyes, the painting took my breath away. It was a masterful piece that depicted the very moment I had chosen Claudia's housewarming present, which was the easel my painting was resting on. As fate would have it, that antique turned out to be owned originally by her great-grandmother, Mary Buchanan.

Claudia put her arm around my shoulder. "You are the first one to lay eyes on this painting. I didn't even let Jake see it yet."

"How on earth did you do this, Claudia?"

Running her hand over the edge of the canvas, she exhaled. "Well, it wasn't easy! The day after you gave me the easel, I went to the antique shop in Perkins Cove. When I told the owner of my plan for this painting, she loved the idea and allowed me to take some pictures of the room where you found the easel. I also remembered that my dad had an old family photo album with pictures of my great-grandmother Mary. I borrowed one of her pictures to paint her into this piece. The rest is history!"

"Claudia, you have no idea! The day she appeared to me in the store, she looked exactly like that. I mean, she was even wearing that dress."

"You know what, Allie? I'm shocked!"

"Shocked that you painted this exactly the way I saw Mary Buchanan?"

"No way! I'm shocked that it doesn't shock me! Wait, did I say that right? Anyway, I think you know what I mean."

A voice behind me pleaded, "*Hey*, did you forget me?"

I spun around to Alex standing in the doorway of the studio.

Claudia reacted to my response and shivered. "Do we have company again?

"We sure do!"

"Geeze, it feels a bit cold in here. Is she causing that?"

Without waiting for my response, Claudia left the room and headed down the hallway. "Tell her I said hello. I'm jumping in the shower."

As she strolled down to the bathroom, I yelled, "You can tell her yourself, you know! She can hear you even if you can't hear her."

When I looked back, Alex was not there. "Where are you now?"

Her voice called out from the great room. "I'm in here."

I stepped out of the studio. "If you want to talk to me, you can't just bounce from room to room."

She became annoyed, and placing her hands on her hips, she grunted. "I can't control it. I think you have more power over where I am any given time than I do. It seems that I find myself in your presence at your every beck and call."

"What does that mean?"

"I thought I was here so you could help me figure out who killed me, but I'm starting to question that now."

When Alex vanished again, I couldn't help but laugh. "Alex, would you stop that?"

Her voice rang out from the kitchen. "Well, if you don't care to know what I have to say, I guess I'll just have to hang around until you do; because I am here for *you* this time."

I moved to the kitchen doorway and stood there, confused by this bizarre exchange. "Seriously, Alex, what could you possibly have to say that might help me?"

"I need to tell you that someone is following you, and they're always just beyond your view all the time."

"What? You have seen someone following me?"

"Well, yes, and I can't seem to get a good look at their face. When I try to approach them, I find myself back in your presence."

Again, she evaporated into thin air. This time, when I called out to her, there was no response. So, what in tarnation was I to do with that? I already knew that Makya was likely lurking around every corner. How was this to help me? Moving to the cabinet, I grabbed the bottle of Tylenol and a glass.

Showered, Claudia came back to the kitchen as I broke the seal on the Tylenol bottle. "Got a headache?"

"Splitting headache is more like it. I feel like someone is drilling my skull with a jackhammer from the inside out."

"You need to get some sleep, Allie. I think we both do."

"Swallowing the pills, I placed my glass in the dishwasher. "I'm going to shower and go right to bed."

As I left the kitchen, Claudia asked, "So is Alex gone?"

I echoed back, "For now!"

Chapter 23

I didn't have the strength to linger in the shower long. I was just too tired. I was in bed in less than ten minutes and was asleep so quickly, I barely remember putting my head down on the pillow.

I must have been sleeping for a couple of hours when suddenly someone was pinning me down to the bed and covering my mouth, muffling my screams.

Thrashing, I struggled to break free, but his grasp stifled my voice.

He rolled me over and whispered, "Shhh! Shhh!"

Was I dreaming? No, I wasn't, and when I opened my eyes, Josh's face came into focus.

"Oh, my God, you're here! You're really here!"

My heart was racing as he embraced me, and I thought I would pass out from sheer exuberance. As he ran his hands through my hair to push it away from my face, he gave me the deepest kiss; I thought he would devour me. I pushed him away enough to tear open his shirt, popping every button as

I pulled it from his body. I unzipped his jeans, shoved them down past his hips, and hooked them with my feet, struggling to pull them away from his legs. Josh pulled me up in his arms, sliding my nightgown up over my head and tossing it to the floor. Finally, there it was, that familiar feeling of my body racked with sensations too intense to even describe. Neither of us could speak as we melted into the moment and became drained by the experience.

Falling against me with sheer contentment, Josh whispered, "I couldn't wait another minute, not even another second to hold you."

Wrapped in an embrace, we lay there, staring at each other. With my fingers, I traced my hand over Josh's face. "Please tell me I'm not dreaming, that you are really here. This isn't some altered state of mine that I've slipped into, is it?"

"No, Allie, I'm here, and I am going to stay here with you. I am not leaving your side again."

"Josh, I don't understand; where have you been?"

He placed his hand over my mouth. "Can we just bask in this moment?"

I was growing fearful. "I'm afraid I'm dreaming. Lately, I feel like I am moving from one reality to another. What is real? What is not real? If this is a dream, I don't want to wake up!"

He slid his hand down from my neck to my side and then down my thigh. Pulling my leg up and around him, he kissed me and whispered, "I'm here, Allie. I am really here!"

Not wanting to break the spell, I lay there motionless in his embrace until I felt him sitting up. Reaching out, I grabbed his arm. "Josh, where are you going?"

"I'm not going anywhere. I thought you were sleeping."

"I can't sleep. I'm afraid to fall asleep. I'm so scared that when I wake up, you will be gone."

Pulling me up in the bed and back into his arms, he continued to reassure me. "Allie, honey, I'm here. I'm not going anywhere."

I couldn't wait any longer. I needed some answers. "Josh, can you please tell me where you have been? Why haven't you contacted me? Why would you let me believe all this time that you might be dead? Why would you let me think that you just vanished without a trace?"

Pulling me closer, he gently kissed my forehead. "Allie, I had to stay away to keep you safe."

Sitting forward, I turned in his direction. "Just tell me what happened. Start by explaining what happened that night you disappeared."

He eased away from me, climbed out of bed, picked up his jeans, and slid them on. "Well, I guess that is as good a place as any to start. When I came down to your apartment to retrieve my checkbook that evening, I found the door just slightly ajar. When I walked into the foyer, I remember thinking how careless it was for us to leave the door open like that. I came to your room, grabbed my checkbook, and started back out to the great room when I heard a noise coming from somewhere else in the apartment. I went to the kitchen and grabbed a knife out of the block on the counter. Making my way to Claudia's studio, there was no one there, so I returned to the great room, and as I did, I was shoved from behind. I spun around and struck out with the knife. I could feel it make contact with my assailant, and I heard him gasp. He grabbed my arm and shoved the knife up toward my face, missing me, lodging the blade in the wall behind my head. We continued to struggle and fight, moving from room to room. He grabbed a large lamp off one of the end tables and struck me, catching both my knees, and I dropped to the floor. He continued pummeling me with the light until I managed to grab it, taking it from his grip. I was so enraged I could feel the adrenalin pumping through my body. I took the lamp and blindly struck out at him. I managed to grab his leg and bring him to the floor when I heard his cell phone buzz. As we continued to struggle, he removed it from his pocket and drew it to his face. He grunted and drove his free leg into my head. That's the last thing I remember before passing out."

Climbing from the bed, I draped my arms around his neck. "How on earth did you get away then?"

"Well, I didn't exactly getaway, but he did. I woke up hours later in a hospital bed."

"What?"

"God, Allie, this is so complicated, but suffice it to say that I was taken into protective custody. I wasn't allowed to contact anyone, not even you."

"What? Did Payne know about this?"

"No, not even Payne knew about it."

"Does he now?"

"He will in the morning because I am going to the station with you to talk to him."

I slid around and stood behind Josh. "I don't know why you felt the need to put these jeans back on." Wrapping my hands around his waist, I unzipped them for the second time and pulled them to the floor.

He stepped out of them, turned to me, and scooped me up in his arms. "I missed this most of all, Allie."

Falling into bed, we lingered and enjoyed every sensation and vibration in our bodies until we fell asleep from physical exhaustion.

During the night, I felt myself floating, and before I knew what was happening, I was riding on that familiar horse, swept up by the sweet smell of the grass in the breeze. It was so tall; I felt it brushing against my bare feet as we galloped through a field. A young man was standing next to a gallant black horse that glistened as the sun hit its coat in the near distance. As we drew closer, it became increasingly clear that he was not a stranger to me. Stopping, something compelled me to climb down and move toward him. Looking up into his face, it was the eyes that I recognized. It was me standing there in front of him, but strangely, I felt disconnected from my body. As he reached over and touched my face, I felt my body being catapulted, like a slingshot had shot me into space.

Suddenly, like a hard landing, I was sucked back into my body and shaken awake. Afraid to even open my eyes, I reached out, frantically searching, only to find the other side of the bed empty. Was this all a dream? What just happened? Suddenly I remembered something. Something I had just dreamed. The young man I just came across in my dream was from a different era, but those eyes, those beautiful blue eyes, they belonged to Josh!

I sat up and stared around the room, and to my relief, Josh's jeans were there on the floor, right where he stepped out of them the night before. He emerged from the bathroom, drying his hair with a towel wrapped around his waist.

My mind was racing as I blurted, "I'm so glad to see you!"

"Well, good morning, sleepyhead! I told you I wasn't going anywhere. I've already showered, but I'll gladly join you in there. You can never be too clean, you know!"

"No, let me take a quick shower; we have a lot of explaining to do today. Claudia is going to freak when she sees you. And just wait until my mother lays eyes on you."

"Allie, Claudia is one thing, but before we start announcing my arrival, we need to talk to Payne. One of the conditions of my leaving protective custody was that I lie low until I have a chance to reach out to the local law enforcement."

"Wait, let me get this straight. Am I the only one that knows that you're back? How did you get in here last night without anyone knowing?"

There it was, that Cheshire cat grin of his that I loved so much. "I didn't say you were the only one who knows I'm here."

Standing a little taller, I turned my head in his direction. "Who else knows? And just how long have they known?"

"There's one other person who knows, and that's Dakota. I knew I couldn't get up here unseen without his help. Of course, we will have to tell Antonio this morning because we won't get past him at the door without him knowing."

Grabbing some clothes from the closet, I headed to the shower. "Okay, give me a few minutes, and then we'll go talk to Claudia."

I stepped into the bathroom to find Alex sitting on the vanity. "Allie, that's the guy who was following you."

"Alex, we really have to establish some boundaries here."

"But, didn't you hear me? That's the guy I saw following you."

"I'm sure he was. That is Josh, my fiancé. Look, I don't have time to explain, but he's fine. I'm glad that is who you saw; he is not a threat."

"If you say so?"

Before I could respond, she, once again, evaporated into thin air.

Chapter 24

I was in and out of the shower in record time. Coming out of the bathroom, I ran to Josh, wrapping my arms around his neck. I took a deep breath. "I still can't believe you're here."

Moving to the nightstand, I picked up my Apple watch and placed it on my wrist, and then sat on the bed to put on my sneakers. "Josh, why don't you give me a minute with Claudia so I can prepare her."

"Sure, that's fine; after all, this is going to be one hell of a surprise."

Stepping out of the room, I made my way to the kitchen. "Good morning, Claudia. How did you sleep last night?"

Rolling her eyes, she sighed. "Like a rock! My head hit the pillow, and I didn't hear one more thing all night until my alarm went off this morning."

I placed a cup in the Keurig coffee maker and selected the button for the tallest cup of coffee. "Well, I was pretty busy last night. I didn't get much sleep at all!"

She tipped her head from side to side, looking at me inquisitively. "What? What are you talking about? Oh no, was it Alex? Did she keep you up all night? Next time she's around, you just let me know! I'll let her have it!"

"No, Claudia, it wasn't Alex."

Josh stepped into the doorway. "Hey, how about a coffee for me?"

Stunned, she dropped her plate of toast on the floor. "OMG, you're here! Where the heck did you come from? I mean, where have you been?" As she kneeled to pick up her toast, she never took her eyes off of Josh.

Josh rushed to help. "Here, let me get that. I'm so sorry."

Standing slightly, she reacted. "I don't know if I want to kiss you or let you have it! We have been so worried for months. What the heck, Josh?"

"I know. I'm so sorry."

Stepping over to help them pick up the rest of the toast, I interrupted. "Wait, Claudia, you need to hear him out. It wasn't his fault. He was taken into protective custody."

"Protective custody? Are you kidding me?"

She stood to face Josh. "Do you mean Payne knew you were alive all this time and let us all think you might be dead?"

"No, he had no idea what had happened to me. That night the FBI was there. They arrived at the scene and extracted me before Payne, or anyone else, got there. They were in and out before anyone realized what happened. There is way more to this whole Makya case than Payne or anyone outside of the FBI even knows about."

Claudia moved to the chair at the island and sat down as the whole thing sank in. "So, that was you we saw at the hospital yesterday. I just knew it. Oh, my God, we have so many questions. The first one being, why the hell did they keep you from us all this time? We have all been worried to death! Jake and I had to get married without you there standing up for him."

Josh stepped over to Claudia and gave her a gentle hug. "I know. I am so sorry. I do have a lot of explaining to do, but for now, I would just love to have some breakfast with my two favorite women."

Looking up at Josh, she smiled as a tear fell down her cheek. "Of course. What would you like? I have cut up some fresh fruit, and I could make some eggs and toast?"

I pulled the fruit from the refrigerator. "Why don't we just have some coffee, toast, and fruit?"

Josh took a seat at the counter. "I'll second that."

While I got the fruit and coffee ready, Claudia made some more toast. "Would anyone like cinnamon or jam?"

When Claudia and I joined Josh at the island, I reached over and put my hand on hers. "No one except Dakota, you, and I know Josh is back. We will have to tell Antonio, but we need to keep this on the down-low, at least until we have filled Payne in."

"But, Al, can I tell Jake?"

"Of course. I thought after we talk to Payne today, Josh and I could come to the hospital and surprise Jake. That reminds me, we need to talk to Antonio. Let me go get him, and we can feed him and break the news about Josh."

Getting up, I moved to the apartment entrance. I stepped into the foyer and stood directly in front of Antonio. "How about some coffee and something to eat?"

Rolling his eyes, he smirked. "I thought you would never ask. I'm starving!"

"Well, come in and join us. We have something to tell you." Before we got to the kitchen, I stopped. "Prepare yourself. This is going to be a bit of a shock."

Josh stepped out into the great room. "Hey there, Antonio, it's great to see you, pal!"

Antonio gasped. "Holy shit, where did you come from?" As Josh stepped forward to shake his hand, Antonio smirked. "The hell with that." He pulled Josh in for a man hug and patted him on the back. "Oh, my God, I can't believe it! Where the hell have you been?"

I gave them both a little shove. "Come on, we'll fill you in over breakfast."

Chapter 25

When we left the Summit that morning, and to avoid running into anyone, Antonio, Josh, and I took the elevator directly to the parking garage. Leading Josh over to Dakota's convertible, I clicked the remote and unlocked the doors. "Let's take this." We all climbed in, and much to my surprise, Josh didn't even blink. As I put the key into the ignition, I turned to him. "Aren't you going to ask me why I'm driving Dakota's car?"

"No, don't forget, Allie. I have been back and observing you for about a week. I can't believe I managed to avoid your seeing me this entire time. Well, until that close call yesterday."

"Josh, let me remind you that I thought you might be dead, and I wasn't exactly expecting you to pop up anywhere, least of all in the apartment. I was too busy looking for Makya; he is high on my radar."

Pulling out of the parking garage, with Antonio following us, we headed to the station. En route, I called Payne on his office phone. He answered on the third ring.

"Hello, Detective Payne here."

"Hi, Payne, it's Allie. I am on my way to the station. I need to talk to you about something. Can I meet you in your office this morning as soon as I get there?"

"Sure thing, what's so urgent?"

"I think this is something I need to tell you face-to-face."

"Okay then, just come right up when you get here. I'll be waiting. Did you get an access badge yet?"

"Yes, I was issued one yesterday. Good, see you in a few."

At the station, Stacy greeted us. "Good morning, Allie. Congratulations on your new position here. Welcome aboard!"

Josh mumbled under his breath. "New position here? Now that I didn't know about. What exactly does that mean?"

I ignored him. "Thank you. I am looking forward to working with all of you. We're headed up to Payne's office."

"Certainly, no problem. Have a great day!"

Approaching Payne's office, I turned to Josh. "Are you ready for this?"

"Oh, I certainly am!"

Payne had his back to the door when we walked in. Without turning around, he raised his hand, motioning that he would be right with us. Finishing his conversation, he turned to put down his phone. "Okay, George, we'll come down to the war room in just a few minutes."

The shock on his face as he looked up was almost immeasurable. He immediately moved out from behind the desk, offering Josh his hand, and then pulled him in to embrace him. "Well, for the love of God, where did you come from? We have been looking all over tarnation for you, son! I don't know if I should be happy to see you or angry that you have let us worry all this time about your fate."

"I'm sorry, Payne, I do have a lot of explaining to do, but the bottom line is that I was in protective custody. I wasn't permitted to contact anyone until now. As it turns out, we weren't the only one with our sights on Makya."

"Well, I guess that explains why I received a message from someone at the FBI late last night. I was just about to return his call. Why don't both of you head down to the war room, and I'll join you as soon as I can. Clearly, I need to be brought up to speed."

Josh and I left the office and headed down the hall. Just before we got to the war room, I stopped, grabbing his arm. "Josh? There's something I should tell you before we meet with the others."

Looking a little puzzled, he stroked the side of my face. "Okay, what is it?"

"Ah…I need to tell you about the new task team Payne brought together that is now working on our case. I mean, you know most everyone on the team. It includes Detectives Carl Johnson from New York and Hayln Deere from Colorado, as well as Brian Davis from forensics. George and Dakota are helping with the research on the investigation as well, but there is one more person you should know about. Ah, I don't know quite how to say this, but I want you to keep an open mind."

Josh winced, closing one eye. "Just spill it, Allie!"

"It's Delsin Hill."

Josh's face turned crimson red. "Are you kidding me? This guy has some culpability in this case. He is partially responsible for what is happening!"

I stepped in front of Josh to block him from moving another step. "I thought that, too, at first, but just hear me out on this."

"What's to hear? I don't get it. I can't believe Payne let him anywhere near this case, let alone in any proximity of you!"

Placing both hands on his chest, I could feel his heart pounding through his shirt. "Josh, this is not like you at all. Please hear him out when you meet him. It's not at all what you think."

I no sooner got the words out when Payne came around the corner and jetted past us in the hallway, barking, "Come on, you two, we've got to move on from this Delsin Hill issue. Right now, we've got much bigger fish to fry than him!"

Chapter 26

Following Payne into the war room, I spoke to Josh under my breath. "Hey, you need to let us get you up to speed before you rush to judgment about Delsin."

"I don't promise anything right now, except that I will hear him out."

The shock of the group was palpable as we walked into the room with Josh. George stood from the conference table, opened his mouth, but was tongue-tied.

Payne chimed in. "I've got information to share with this group, but it's undeniable that we need to deal with the fact that Josh is here with us first. Actually, what I have learned in the past ten minutes is related to his return. Please, could everyone take a seat so I can bring you all up to speed?"

Delsin moved over and took a seat next to Josh, extending his hand to him. "Please let me introduce myself. My name is Delsin Hill."

Josh did not offer his hand. "Yes, Allie told me you would be here, and since you're the only person in this room I didn't recognize, it wasn't hard to figure out who you were. Not to be rude, but I have to be honest, I am not really clear why you have been brought in to work with us."

Withdrawing his hand, Delsin shook his head. "That's fair. I would feel the same if I were in your shoes. I'll tell you the same thing I told Allie. I am so sorry we're meeting under these circumstances. Look, Josh, while I was inside, I spent a year with Makya. He used our Native American backgrounds to gain my trust. Makya told me that his father was a medicine man and an influential member of his tribe. As time went on, we shared more and more about our families, but for some reason, I never quite trusted him enough to talk about exactly what tribe I was from. Once he learned about the elders' disagreement over the ancestral box, he started to show his true colors. When I refused to give him Allie's or her grandfather's names, he grew increasingly unpredictable and aggressive. I was relieved that I was released when I was. I couldn't get away from him fast enough. I made certain that when I left prison, I didn't tell any of the inmates where I was headed. Believe me, I wanted to put that whole experience behind me. I had no idea how powerful and gifted Makya was or about his insatiable thirst for power until he no longer had use for me. Only then did I realize how dangerous he was."

Payne interrupted. "Look, I have a great deal to go over with everyone." He stretched his neck from side to side, releasing the tension. "We need to get past this issue just for now and get down to business. God, I'm not sure really where to begin. Before I came down here to meet with you, I returned a call to a gentleman named James Currie from the FBI. He will be here tomorrow morning to join us in this investigation. It appears we aren't the only organization after the infamous Makya. The FBI has been following him and his escapades across the country and they were still pursuing him when he arrived here in Maine. In fact, they were at the Summit the night Josh disappeared. I now know, that they got on the scene before we did, extracted Josh and put him into protective custody. They did not want to expose their own investigation at that time. According to Agent Currie, Makya has left far more carnage behind him than we even knew about—a trail of thirty additional bodies in his wake from Los Angeles to Maine. Most of them were very bizarre killings, but they all had one thing in common." Standing, Payne pivoted towards me. "They were all slit from ear to ear, but that was never the cause of their death."

I shot back at him. "Alex!" Just like Alex!"

"Yes, just like Alex."

Turning to Payne, Dakota winced. "Who is Alex?"

"Alex is a young woman that was brought into the morgue this week. We probably would never have connected her to Makya if we didn't have this new information. Alex just happens to be the daughter of a technician in our forensics lab and the wife of Arthur Stevens, the assistant district attorney.

"That is where the story gets even more bizarre. All of those victims we didn't know about were kept off the radar.

The FBI kept them as quiet as possible. Each of those victims had a connection to someone on the police force or agency that was investigating Makya. Even stranger, they weren't all actively involved in the case but worked with those who were. The victims were somewhat random and seemed to just be peripheral damage, bringing me to Josh. The FBI felt he was another one of the victims they put in that category. Josh was taken into protective custody for his own protection. Makya doesn't know if Josh actually survived his attack in the apartment that night."

Brian got up from his seat and paced. "I don't get it; there has to be some connection between those victims and Makya. Why would he randomly go after anyone who wasn't connected to the investigation? Josh wasn't just peripheral damage, he was very much involved in the case, yet the FBI considered him one of that group of victims. Payne, we really need to see the case files and forensic reports from their investigation."

Payne got up to move to the whiteboards. "I'm sure we will have access to that information when we meet with Agent Currie tomorrow. I guess we had better rearrange these boards so we can add the notes on the additional cases to what we already have here."

Brian got up and headed for the door. "I think I am going to return to the morgue and go over what we have on Alex's case again. I'll let you all know if I come up with anything."

My phone buzzed. "Payne, this is Claudia. I need to call her. I'll be right back."

Stepping out of the room, I dialed Claudia's number. When she answered, she sounded a little strange and nervous. "Allie, where are you?"

"I'm at the police station. What's going on?"

"It's Jake. The doctor said he wants to keep him under observation, run a few more tests, and then discharge him in a few days!"

I released a great sigh of relief. "That's great. That means he's doing better. That's the best news, Claudia!"

"Is it? Don't you think it's a little too soon? I mean, it seems a little soon to me."

"Claudia, he's not sending Jake back to work. He's just discharging him from the hospital. I'm sure he will have to take it easy for a while. Besides, when he does go back to work, Payne wants him tied to my hip to keep me out of trouble. Look, Claudia, he's practically tied our hands behind our backs with all the terms he's given us to work on this case together."

After a long silence, she finally replied, "I guess you're right."

"Look, as soon as Josh and I leave here, we are heading over to the hospital. Have you said anything to Jake about Josh?"

"No, not yet. Do you think I should?"

I thought for a second. "Although I am sure he will be glad to see Josh, it might be a bit of a shock if you don't prepare him first."

"You're right. I'll talk to him about it before you get here."

Returning to the war room, I went directly to Payne. "Claudia said they are going to release Jake in a few days."

"That's great!"

"Thank you. That is exactly what I said, but Claudia was a little concerned. She thought it might be a little soon."

"Look, Allie, I thought maybe you, Josh, and I could leave and go over to the hospital to see Jake now. What do you say?"

"I think that's a great idea."

"Are you kidding me? Why aren't you joining Brian down in the morgue? You just learned that my death is somehow connected to your case. Aren't you even a little curious about that? I mean, it is becoming increasingly clear that the reason you can see me has as much to do with your case as it does mine. It's becoming increasingly clear that I am here to help you as much as you are meant to help figure out what happened to me!"

I spun around to see Alex. "Come on, can you please be a little patient? I know this must be upsetting, but it has only been a couple of days. We're going to get this guy, I promise!"

From about five feet away, Dakota responded, "What?"

"Oh, sorry, not you. It was Alex."

Dakota looked puzzled as Payne piped in. "Can I assume we have company? I mean company none of the rest of us can see?"

"Yes, but she's gone now. Sorry, Payne, but she is a little upset that we are leaving and not working with Brian down in the morgue this afternoon."

As we left the war room, Payne placed a call on his cell. "Hello Antonio, I am going to follow Allie and Josh over to Southern Maine Medical in the squad car. Could you please meet them over there to start your shift and then escort them home from there?" Payne motioned for us to follow him down the hall to his office.

By the time we got to his office, Payne was off his phone. He turned to both of us and said, "How would Claudia say it? "Let's leave this Hoodsie stand?"

I was really amused by the fact that he was trying to quote Claudia, but couldn't let it go without correcting him. "That's a good try, but her expression is 'Let's blow this Hoodsie stand!'"

Laughing, he picked up his keys. "Alrighty then, Let's blow this Hoodsie stand!"

Chapter 27

Walking into the parking lot, I took my keys from my bag and handed them to Josh. "Do you mind driving? I'm going to call Claudia to make sure she has been able to talk to Jake before we descend on them."

Josh took my keys, unlocked the doors with the key fob, and we climbed in. Pulling out of the parking space, Payne moved in behind us in his car to follow us.

Dialing Claudia, she answered on the second ring.

"Hi, Allie!"

"Hey, Claudia. I just wanted to call and give you a heads-up. We're on our way. Have you had a chance to talk to Jake?"

"As a matter of fact, I have, and he has been waiting, not so patiently, for you both to get here."

I heard Jake in the background. "What the hell is taking them so long? Tell them to put on the siren and get the heck over here."

I could hear new energy in his voice. "Well, it sounds like he's feeling better! Tell him to keep his johnny on! Let him know we are on our way and we're in Dakota's car, which, incidentally, does not have a siren. We're about fifteen minutes out."

Twenty minutes later, as we approached Jake's room, we heard a great deal of laughter. Just before we entered, I heard Claudia.

"Hey, wait, everyone, I need to tell you something!"

She no sooner got the words out when Josh, Payne, and I walked into the room.

Claudia turned to us. "Well, I guess the cat's out of the bag now."

Standing next to the bed were Claudia's father, Bill, my mother, and Guile. They all just stood there, looking like deer in the headlights of a Mack truck. No one could speak.

Finally, I cut through the shock of everyone by breaking the silence. "Well, I guess you must all be surprised with our new development."

Dropping her handbag on the edge of Jake's bet, Mom rushed over and wrapped her arms around Josh. "Oh, my God! Oh my, God! You're here." Stepping back, she reached up and caressed his cheeks. "You really are a sight for sore eyes, son."

Guile and Bill rushed over and embraced Josh. Everyone was so elated to see him.

Bill finally stepped back. "Where the heck have you been, Josh?"

"Well, sir, that's kind of a long story, but I'm not sure if I am at liberty to share everything right now."

Payne interjected. "Let me just say that Josh is smack dab in the middle of one hell of an investigation, and right now, we can't discuss anything. In fact, very few people even know he is back. Not even his family have been notified yet.".

Reaching over, wrapping her arm around my shoulder, Mom caught her breath. "Oh, my God, Allie, this is wonderful. I am so glad to see Josh back safe and sound."

Jake waved his arms in the air to get our attention from his hospital bed. "Hey, over here! Did you all forget about me?"

Josh broke from the group and moved over to Jake. "Hey, buddy! You're lookin' a little rough around the edges! Looks like you've been having a hard time staying out of the line of fire lately!"

Jake and Josh fist-bumped.

"That is probably a pretty accurate statement! Both figuratively and literally!"

Payne moved over to Jake and offered his hand. "I, for one, am so glad you are awake and feeling better, my friend. We need you back at work, but not until you are one hundred percent. I don't know if you have heard, but you have a new rookie partner."

"Yes, I did hear a rumor to that effect!"

About an hour later, Payne looked at his watch and excused himself. "I think I'll be heading back over to the station and let you all catch up."

As Payne left the room, Mom reached over to hug Jake. "I think we'll be going as well. Guile promised to take Bill and me to a late lunch." She gave each of us a kiss on the cheek. "Do you think the four of you can stay out of trouble for just a little while?"

Josh wrapped his arm around my waist, pulling me to his side. "I sure hope so."

As they left the room, each of us pulled chairs up next to Jake's bed, and I heard Alex's all too familiar voice. "Do you think I could hang with you guys for a while?"

She was standing right behind Claudia.

"Hey, girl, you're back." I tried to make light of the situation and chuckled. "Sure, the more, the merrier!"

Everyone just looked on in amazement as Alex and I conversed.

As she spoke, a sadness swept over her face. "I don't know how long I can stay with you here. I feel like I am no longer tethered to this physical world. Like I'm a helium balloon that slipped off of its string. I'm just floating around aimlessly with the whim of every breeze that comes along. I haven't quite figured out how to move through this new existence of mine yet. It seems like I move from location to location at someone else's will. When someone needs me, I can almost hear them calling out, and then I find myself in their presence."

I suddenly felt awful about joking with her. "I'm so sorry! I guess boundaries are out of the question until we figure this all out."

Claudia couldn't contain herself. "Allie, that's Alex, isn't it?"

"Yes, I think I just hurt her feelings."

"Is she still here?"

"Ah, yes, and she wants to hang around with us for a while!"

"Is she right behind me? I can feel the coolness in the air."

"Yes, she is."

Claudia turned and faced the opposite direction. "Like, right here?"

"Yes, she is standing right there."

Confidently, without hesitation, Claudia began speaking. "Look, Alex, I wish I could reach out and hug you to make you feel better or something, but that's clearly not possible. Of course, you can hang out with us, at least until we figure out who did this to you. My guess is that you would be happier moving on to where you are really supposed to be. Like, to the light or something. Maybe Allie can help you with that also."

A look of relief washed over Alex's face. "Allie, please thank Claudia for me. I wish I knew you both before all this happened. Oops, I have to go. I'm sure I will be back." With that, she disappeared again.

For the next few hours, the four of us spent time catching up and reminiscing.

About eight-thirty, the nurse walked in. "I hate being the time police, but visiting hours were over a half-hour ago, and it's my job to be the bearer of that bad news."

As she turned and walked out of the room, the three of us got up from our chairs. Leaning in, Claudia kissed Jake.

"We've got to go, honey. We don't want to wear out our welcome here. Besides, you'll be home soon, and we'll have plenty of time to visit.

"You're right, but just one more thing before you all leave. Josh, where are you and Allie staying now that you are back?"

"To be honest, I don't think either of us has had time to even think about that."

Jake extended his hand for Josh to shake. "I would be really grateful if the two of you would stay at the apartment for a while. We have plenty of room. I know Antonio is stationed there at night, but I would feel much better if you were there as well."

"That would be great, but as newlyweds, that might just cramp your style. Don't you think?"

Claudia burst out laughing. "I think our privacy is on hold for right now, between our living and non-living friends popping in and out. I think I heard someone say a little while ago, the more, the merrier! Right, Allie?"

Moving over to stand in solidarity with Claudia, I chimed in. "I'm in. How about you, Josh?"

"I'm in. We certainly need a place to lay our heads until we can make other arrangements. Well, since I lost my apartment while I was gone, I either need to stay with all of you or sleep at the dojo. I do have to say, the apartment sounds like a much better option!"

Chapter 28

Antonio, Josh, Claudia, and I arrived at the Summit that evening at nine-thirty. Sandy greeted us from the front desk. "Good evening, you guys! I have a message for you from Dakota. He asked me to have one of you call him when you got in this evening."

As we approached the desk, I leaned over the counter and hung my head in my hands. "Josh, honey, do you think you could call him? I'm so tired, I don't think I can even string two thoughts together, much less have a conversation. I've got to get some sleep!"

Claudia chimed in. "Same here. I don't think I can keep my eyes open much longer. I have been in fight-or-flight mode since the shooting. I think the adrenalin has drained all the energy from my body, leaving me feeling weak and exhausted. Like I've run a weeklong marathon and used up all the energy in my body."

Wrapping his arm around my shoulder, Josh led me to the elevator, and as we stepped in, he held the door open and called back to Sandy. "I'll call Dakota, just as soon as Antonio and I get these two upstairs and safely tucked in for the night."

When we got to the apartment, Antonio went in first. "Okay, guys, it's clear, come on in."

Josh brought me straight to the bedroom, pulled back the covers, and, taking me by the shoulders, sat me down gently on the bed. Kneeling, he removed my shoes and socks. He helped me slide out of my clothes and tucked me in. "Okay, Allie, it's time for some much-needed sleep." I think I was asleep almost before my head even hit the pillow.

A few hours later, there was a loud crash that shook me to my core. I woke up, laying in tall grass surrounded by the cold night air. *Oh, my God, not again!* The darkness made it difficult to see anything, but the light of the moon shone down through the trees, reflecting off something shiny about ten feet away. I dragged myself over to see what it was and found that it was a suit of armor. I reached over to lift the face shield back, but it was dented and jammed shut.

A voice cried out from inside the armor. "Ainsley, get out of here! Go, before someone sees you!"

I was beyond confused. "What? Ainsley?"

"Are you not Ainsley?"

Before I could even answer, I felt the sensation of being catapulted forward and fell to the ground for a second time. Laying there, I lifted my head. I was back in the woods next to the campfire with Catori. This time, though, she was with

Grandfather. Running to him, I threw myself into his arms. "Grandfather! Oh, Grandfather, I am so scared and confused!"

As he cradled me in his arms, I couldn't stop sobbing.

"There, there, my little bird. You must go back."

"Go back where? I'm not even sure where I belong anymore. The lines are beginning to blur. I have no idea what is real anymore or where I am really supposed to be!"

He gently put his hands on my cheeks, wiping my tears with his thumbs. "I know you're frightened, my little one, but hear me. Find the dream catcher with the tree of life in the center and wear it on your neck always. It will serve to remind you that the roots of the tree will ground you and you will always return to your true time and life. The more you become one with the elements, the more you need to learn how to remain grounded."

With a start, I sat straight up in the bed, gasping for air. I felt like I had run a marathon. Josh reached out and caught my arm. "Allie, you're okay. You were dreaming."

"No Josh, I need to get the ancestral box. I need to call Dakota and get it right away."

Getting up, he threw on his robe. "All right, Allie, what's going on?"

"I know this sounds crazy, but Grandfather just came to me. There is a necklace in the box. I need to get it and put it on."

"What? What are you talking about? I mean, I don't doubt you for a second, but can this wait until morning? It's two a.m."

"I don't think so. Did you call Dakota earlier? Were you able to talk to him?"

"Yes, Allie, but he just wanted an update on Jake."

"I know this sounds nuts, but Josh, I need that box right now. I don't think I will be able to sleep another wink until I have it. It must be important if Catori and Grandfather are reaching out to me."

"Okay, Allie, okay! Let me get my cell."

Within ten minutes, Dakota was at the door with the box. We brought it right into the kitchen and sat it on the island. I ran my hand over the lid. "I hope I'm right about this."

Opening the box, I lifted the top shelf to find a small manila envelope resting on the side of the second shelf. Raising it, I poured the contents into my hand. "This is it. This is the dream catcher pendent Grandfather and Catori told me about. Look at the beautiful tree of life in its center. Its roots are as large as the tree is high. Being deeply rooted in the earth keeps the tree grounded and stable."

Gesturing at me, Josh smiled. "May I do the honors?"

I placed it in his hands and turned my back to him. "Yes, please."

The minute he closed the clasp, I felt an overwhelming sense of security and a heaviness in my entire body. At the same time, it was almost like someone took a blindfold from my eyes, and now I could see things more clearly. I turned to Dakota. "Thank you so much for bringing me the box! I'm so sorry for waking you in the middle of the night like this."

"It's okay Allie. I'm going to take the box back upstairs and lock it away again unless there is anything else you think you might need from me."

"No, there's nothing else, at least not now."

Josh took a deep breath. "Well, Allie, do you feel better?"

"Yes, and I suddenly feel tired, but more importantly, I feel more grounded. I know that probably doesn't make sense to either of you, but it makes perfect sense to me. It's like I have been put solidly back where I belong. I think as I learn to pass between dimensions, the lines can begin to get blurred. Where my true time is, can seem unclear. Now I feel centered and deeply rooted here. Kind of like what Alex was saying. Without this necklace, I feel like a balloon that is kept where it belongs because it is tethered to a string that is rooted deeply in the ground on this plane. Strange, huh?"

As Dakota picked up the ancestral box and headed to the door, he chuckled. "I don't understand, but you can try to explain it to me again after we have all gotten some sleep! See you both in a few hours."

Chapter 29

I woke the next morning to the buzzing of my cell phone. Slapping my hand down on it, I slid it off the nightstand to read a text from Payne: *Allie, when you get to the station this morning, come directly to Brian's office.*

Rolling over, I reached for Josh, but he wasn't there. For one split second, I felt panic trying to squeak in. Remembering the events from the night before, I reached up and found the pendant safely clasped around my neck. Sitting up on the edge of the bed, I leaned over and cradled my face in my hands. It seemed like gravity had somehow betrayed me and my body felt like it weighed an extra one hundred pounds.

Right on cue, I heard my grandfather's voice in my head. *You'll get used to that sensation. You are grounded now, my little bird. The pendant will serve to remind you when your feet are firmly planted where you should be.* Looking up, I saw him melt away like a drifting fog.

There was a knock at the door. "Hey, Allie, wake up!" Then, without hesitation, Claudia barged through the door. "Al, it's time to get up!"

Standing, turning in her direction, I wrung out my hands. "What time is it?"

"It's ten o'clock. Josh headed over to the dojo early this morning for a class."

Running around the room to collect my things, I shrieked, "Alone? Did he go alone?"

"No, Allie, relax, of course not. Officer Caswell went with him. Antonio is waiting to escort you and me to the station to see Payne. Josh and Caswell will meet us there."

A little less anxious, I headed into the shower. "Why didn't anyone wake me up?"

As Claudia turned to leave, she laughed. "Well, I guess Josh and Antonio wanted us to both sleep in for a while. To be perfectly honest, Allie, I have only been up a few minutes myself. I'm going to shower and get ready, too."

Antonio, Claudia, and I left the Summit, stopped to get some donuts, and were at the station by ten-forty-five. When we arrived, Josh was walking in with Caswell, so we all went down to the morgue together.

When we walked in, Payne chuckled. "Well, it's nice for you to finally join the living this morning, Allie!"

Turning to him, I smirked. "Okay, enough of the seeing-dead-people humor!"

Brian came out of the back room. "Good morning, Allie. What's that you've got there?"

"Breakfast! Donuts, in fact!

"Cool!"

Reaching into the box, grabbing a donut, he took a huge bite. "Mmm, that's a good donut, and hey, I received Alex's labs back. We got some interesting, although not too surprising results."

Closing the donut box, I smirked. "Wow, you took a bite and got that all out in one breath. I'm impressed."

Payne interjected. "Josh, why don't you and Claudia come with me upstairs to the war room. I want to give them this new information. Antonio, you stay stationed outside Brian's office door. Brian, when you're done here, I want you and Allie to join us in the war room. I would say we have a considerable amount of work to do today."

As Josh and Payne left the room, I waved Brian off and walked over to pour myself a coffee. "Okay, wait! I haven't had any caffeine this morning yet, give me a second."

I guess Brian wasn't in the mood to wait, because he didn't hesitate. "Allie, remember when I told you I didn't believe the cuts on Alex's neck caused her death? Well, I was right! It looks like she was drinking and someone probably slipped her a mickey because she had alcohol and mollies in her system. We also found evidence of a paralyzing drug in her bloodstream. The type they use during surgery, something to stop any voluntary or involuntary movements."

I spun around, showering some of my coffee on the floor. "So, are you saying the cuts on her neck were that clean because she was out cold and paralyzed?"

"No, like I said earlier, I think she was deceased before the cuts were made. Remember, she still had too much blood in her bloodstream. But someone who hadn't thought it through may have staged this to look like that."

Placing my coffee on the table, I began pacing the floor. "I don't know. Makya is pretty smart. He never leaves anything to chance."

Brian stepped in my path, stopping me in my tracks. "Allie, there is something else we found out. The reason I said he may not have thought of it instead of he didn't know better, is because we now have some additional information on Makya."

I shook my head. "No, you're not going to tell me that he was in the medical field, are you?"

"Worse than that, Allie. He was a medical student that got kicked out of his program in his sixth year."

"So, let me guess, he was studying to be a surgeon?"

Brian spun around, picking up some paperwork from his desk, and handed it to me. "He was studying to be a neurosurgeon."

"Oh, my God. What happened?"

"He was kicked out of school and prosecuted for forging scripts. That was only the first time he was incarcerated, but he got out early on a technicality."

"Well, that explains a lot! That's how he knows so much about drugging his victims."

"That's true. So, we aren't just dealing with someone gifted, but someone with enough education in the medical field to be extremely dangerous. Add to that the fact that he has a thirst for power and no conscience and you have the makings of a perfect storm."

Sitting down hard in a chair at the table, I cupped my face in my hands. "Oh, my God! This just keeps getting worse!"

Brian placed his hand on my shoulder. "I choose to look at it as the glass half full. The more we know about this psychopath and what he can do, the better. That is probably the only way we can figure out how to get ahead of him and nail this jerk!"

Sliding the box of donuts over to me, he smiled. "Let's finish our coffee, have a donut, and then go upstairs to join the others."

Chapter 30

When we arrived at the war room twenty minutes later, Antonio, Brian, and I came face-to-face with a surprise: two strangers seated at the conference table.

Before we could react to their presence, Payne waved us in. "Please, come in!"

There were three empty seats on either side of Claudia, so we moved to them and joined the meeting as Payne continued.

"This is Mr. and Mrs. Stevens, Alex's parents."

Suddenly, Alex was standing there between them, pleading with me. "Allie, tell them I'm here! Tell them I love them and that I am okay!"

Trying not to overreact, I stood up from my chair. "May I be excused? I would like to step out of the room for a minute."

By the look on my face, Payne knew something was going on. "Yes, but please take Antonio with you."

Pulling my cell from my pocket as a cover, trying to fake a smile, I responded, "That won't be necessary. I'm just stepping outside the room to make a call."

Payne turned to Antonio and nodded for him to follow me.

As I was hoping, Alex followed me out of the room.

"This is not a good time!"

Stepping back. Antonio raised his hands in a surrender. "I'm just following orders, Allie."

Closing my eyes and shaking my head in frustration, I turned to him. "I'm sorry, I wasn't talking to you."

Shocked at my response, he stepped back a few more steps. "Alrighty then, I'll just stand across the hall and give you some space."

"And when is the right time, Allie? My poor parents are blaming themselves for what happened to me."

"What are you talking about, Alex? They have to know this is not their fault!"

"Allie, I was drawn to them at our home this morning, and I overheard them talking."

"Talking about what?"

"About me! About a call they received before I was abducted!"

"What? Wait, Alex. Slow down! What call?"

"Well, this morning I found myself at home in my parents' kitchen, and I overheard them talking about a call they received the day before I went missing. My mom was crying and blaming herself for my disappearance. She was pounding on my father's chest and yelling at him that they should have taken the caller seriously."

"Alex, this is really important. What did the caller want?"

"I don't know, that's all I heard!"

"Okay! Look, I promise I will have a conversation with your parents as soon as I can, but I really need to get back in there and find out what they are saying to Payne."

I turned to Antonio. "Shall we?"

He rolled his eyes. I'm sure he was just as confused as anyone would be, standing there, watching me talk to thin air. "Sure!"

As we reentered the room, Mr. Stevens said, "We want to help. I'm just not sure what we can do."

Walking to the whiteboard, Payne started to explain. "For the past several months we have been working on a cold case. Well, they're several different cases, but all related to the same perpetrator. He has been leaving a trail of tragedy in his wake for the past ten years. This room is packed with evidence and information regarding his search for Allie, or more specifically something she has in her possession. The investigation actually spans an area across the entire country, from California to Maine. We believe what happened to your daughter is related to this case in some way."

Confused, Mrs. Steven turned to Payne. "How can that be? Our daughter was only twelve years old ten years ago?"

Moving back to his seat, Payne leaned on the back of his chair. "I know, but over the years there have been some peripheral victims that we weren't able to connect to the guy until just recently. We believe your daughter's case might be one of them and could prove to be invaluable to catching this guy.

Mr. Stevens stood from his chair. "Okay, I've had about enough of this. We came here to help with our daughter's case, not some ten-year-old cold case. We're leaving. You can call us when you have some current information regarding our daughter. Until then, please, don't bother contacting us."

As the Stevens moved to leave, I stood and stepped in the doorway, blocking them. "Wait, please wait!"

Turning to Payne, Alex's father barked, "Payne, I'm warning you!"

"I couldn't hold it in any longer. "Mr. Stevens, tell us about the call you got the day before Alex disappeared!"

Spinning again to face me, he stared directly into my eyes. "What?"

"Tell us about that call, you know what I'm talking about!"

He turned to Payne again. "Is this some kind of joke? What is going on? Did you tap my phone or something?"

Mrs. Stevens faced her husband. "Arthur, enough! That's enough. That call was not a prank! Something is definitely going on here and these people need our help to figure it out!"

Turning, Mr. Stevens returned to the conference table with tears streaming down his face. "I can't believe this has happened to my little girl."

I moved over, faced him, and placed my hands on his shoulders. "I have something to tell you, sir, but first, please have a seat."

I handed him a tissue. "I knew about the call because Alex told me."

"What? Are you crazy? What are you talking about?"

"I know this is a lot to absorb, but Alex has been appearing to me since her death. Just before I left the room, she was standing directly behind you and your wife, pleading with me to tell you she was okay and that none of this was your fault. I left the room because I wanted her to follow me, and she did. She was with you before you came here today and overheard you talking about the call. She couldn't tell me what it was about, but she heard you both talking about it."

"What do you mean, she was with us?"

"It's a little hard to explain, but basically, she is in some sort of limbo right now and she hasn't quite figured out how to move on. The only way to explain it is that she finds herself with those she has a connection to when they need her the most. It's sort of like they call out to her and she finds herself in their presence. Apparently, she was compelled or drawn to you both during your conversation about the call. So, please tell us, what was the call about?"

Mrs. Stevens sat down next to her husband, took his hands in hers, and looked in my direction. "Thank you for telling us that, Allie. Somehow, that does make me feel a little better, and I think I can take it from here. There was a call, but we thought it was a prank.

"Recently, we had some friends who received a call from one of those scam artists. You know, the ones who tell you they have kidnapped one of your loved ones and you have to send them a large sum of money or you will never see them again. Well, the scammer said he had their son, Jeremy, who was away at college. Knowing about these types of scams, they immediately called their son and were able to debunk the story right away. When we got the call about Alex, we thought it was just another scam. His demand was so strange. He wanted us to play a game. He told us not to contact the police and gave us two hours to decide if we would play. If we didn't call him back and agree, he said we would never see Alex alive again. When we hung up, we tried to contact Alex on her cell phone and couldn't reach her. We didn't take the call seriously, but two hours and five minutes later our phone rang again. When Arthur answered, the voice on the other end said just two words, '*Too late!*' and hung up. We didn't even have a chance to respond. The phone just went dead."

At that moment I felt like I would lose the donuts and coffee rolling around in my stomach. "I am so sorry, Mr. and Mrs. Stevens, but honestly, you couldn't have known!"

Tears fell from Mrs. Stevens' eyes. "Please, call us Sara and Arthur."

"Okay, then Sara and Arthur, it is. Do you have any idea what he meant by a game?"

"Not exactly. Something about a treasure hunt. We had to follow clues to a treasure chest we would have to locate and obtain to give him in trade for Alex."

My blood began to boil as I turned to Payne. "Well, I guess we know what treasure chest he was looking for, now don't we!"

Claudia had been silent the whole meeting but didn't hold back. "OMG, the ancestral box!"

Chapter 31

We reconvened after lunch. Josh, Claudia, and I arrived back at the war room ten minutes early. By one o'clock, everyone had arrived except Payne. While we were waiting for him, the speakerphone in the center of the table rang. Thinking it might be Payne calling to let us know he was on his way, I answered it.

"Hello?"

When there was no response, I wished I had just let it ring.

Payne walked into the room, and I pointed to the phone, mouthing, *Someone is on the other end.*

He chimed in. "Hello, this is Detective Payne speaking, how can I help you?"

After a long pause, Payne tried again. "Hello?"

"Well, hello, Payne! Can I assume that you have spoken to the Stevens by now?"

"What do you want, Makya?"

"Come on, Payne. Let's not be so cavalier. I think you know exactly who and what I want!"

Payne didn't respond right away.

"Well, Payne, are you still there?"

Payne chuckled. "It's not going to happen. Do you really think we are going to just turn over Allie and the ancestral box?"

"Oh, I know you will!"

Claudia slapped the table. "Why you evil, arrogant, idiot! Do you really think anyone would ever surrender Allie or the box to you? That wouldn't happen in a thousand years! We'll just keep obstructing and disrupting your plans, you'll see!"

"Well, there you are Claudia. I would recognize that sassy little voice anywhere. Isn't that what you have been trying to do so far? And how has that been working for you? You've gotten close, but I have still managed to stay one step ahead of you. Do you really think the Stevens' are the only people around you that I've engaged in my little treasure hunt?"

No one spoke, and after a long and awkward silence, the phone echoed as Makya stood from his chair, sending it crashing to the floor. "Really, Payne? Do you think me that much of a fool? Well, I'm not, and by the way, I learn quite quickly and my plan is to keep you all very busy, finding, protecting, and warding off all those participating in the hunt for the infamous box."

"We're way ahead of you, Makya. We have already sent out a notice to everyone on the force to be on the lookout for your antics."

"Did you really think I hadn't thought of that? The minute my plan with the Stevens' fell through, I went to Plan B. I put out a mighty large reward for the box. Oh yes, and I didn't just send it out to your everyday run-of-the-mill treasure hunters, oh no! I sent the alert out to what amounts to an army of some of the richest and most ruthless men I know. And believe me, they have less of a conscience than I do. Get ready, Payne. You and your little police department are going to be very busy!"

The phone went dead and within seconds the dial tone was blaring from it.

Josh pounded on the conference table. "That son of a bitch! Just who in the hell does he think he is?"

Claudia and I pushed our chairs back from the table as Payne reacted. "Josh, if you can't maintain control over your emotions, you are going to be out of this room and off this case entirely. Even the research side. I was concerned about letting you be here in the first place."

"I'm sorry, Payne. Of course, I know that. This guy just gets more brazen all the time. Just when we think we have gotten ahead of him and his ruthless plans, he escalates to a whole new level."

Shaking my head and raising my hands in frustration, I walked to the whiteboard. "Look, Payne, I'm glad the FBI is joining our investigation. They can help us cast out a larger net and it sounds like we are going to need an army of our own."

"I'm glad you said that, Allie, because Carl and I called them again this morning before we met with the Stevens'.

There has been a slight change of plans and they are now sending an entire team to join us. They will be here in the morning at eight o'clock. In the meantime, let's spend the next couple of hours rearranging the evidence and materials in here so we can integrate what the FBI brings with them into what we have."

As he moved across the room, he called to Josh. "Hey, can you give me a hand here? This is a folding wall and if we open it up, there is a second conference room on the other side with additional whiteboard space and I think we are going to need it."

We took the next couple of hours rearranging and organizing the evidence and materials we had, spreading it out over the two rooms. When we were finished, I stepped back and gazed at the walls. "Well, I hope we left enough space for the feds to add their material. Who knows what they might have?"

Walking to the door, Payne excused himself. "I have a few other things I need to do before I head home, but I think we're done here for the day. We should reconvene in the morning when they arrive. I'm positive it will be a huge undertaking for us to integrate their evidence and for everyone on both sides of this investigation to come up to speed."

Chapter 32

A t five o'clock, Antonio showed up at the station to start his shift and by five-thirty, Claudia, Josh, and I were in the car, ready to head over to visit Jake. Putting the keys in the ignition, I let the car idle, waiting for Antonio to swing around the parking lot to follow us. Seeing him pull up, I hesitated. "Hey, guys, I've got an idea."

"Oh no, what is it?"

Studying Claudia in the rear view mirror, I scoffed. "What is that supposed to mean?"

Josh smirked in amusement. "Well, we all know what happens when you get an idea in your head. It typically ends up in us getting in some sort of trouble and it is usually with Payne."

I sat a little taller in my seat and turned my head just slightly. "Well, that might be true, but it's not that kind of idea. I've been thinking it might be nice to get Jake something to eat at George's and take it to him. I'm sure he must be tired of the cafeteria food by now."

Beating Claudia to the punch, Josh stretched his hands over his head. "Well, I think that's a great idea! One I think both of us can get behind. What do you say, Claudia?"

Leaning forward, she slapped his hands. "Well, I don't see how that could get us into any trouble. I'm in!"

I called Antonio on my cell. "Hey, I just want to give you a heads-up that we're going to make a quick stop to pick up some food."

"Okay, I'll be right behind you."

We made our way across town and I parked the car in front of George's Café, and Antonio pulled in and parked right behind me. As I went to get out of the car, the driver's door locked. Hitting the auto button on the door, I unlocked it. As soon as I reached for the handle, the door locked again.

I was growing frustrated as Antonio approached the car.

I tried again. "What the heck is wrong with this lock?"

I hit the button twice to unlock all the doors, but this time, they all locked again immediately.

Antonio looked baffled. "What's going on?"

I rolled down the window. "I don't know. It's these darn locks!"

Claudia leaned forward. "What the hell, Allie?"

My cell rang, and as I picked it up, I check the caller ID. "Crap, it says unknown!"

Even before I answered it, I knew in my gut I was going to be sorry!

The voice on the other end was firm. "So, can't get out of your car, huh?"

I could feel nothing but anger swelling up from my core, but I knew I needed to remain calm. I paused long enough to reign in my emotions. "Well, well, Makya. Are you still relying on your gifts to keep your distance from me? Are you afraid to confront me face-to-face? What's your problem?"

Suddenly, I remembered something. It was a flashback, and after a long silence, I got an idea. "Are you still there? You are such a coward! What's the matter, Calian? Do you think your little squaw has become more powerful than you? Do you think I'm done gathering your berries and healing herbs? Come on, you son of a bitch, talk to me!"

That was it. I'd struck a core.

"So, you've done it! That's where you were all those months you dropped off the radar."

Josh took the phone. "What the hell are you talking about?"

There was another long silence, but when Makya began speaking again, there was a distinct change in his tone. It bellowed with evil gratification. "So, you're both back! Josh, you clever little devil, where have you been? I thought you were out of the picture for sure!"

"In your dreams, asshole!"

Makya growled. "Oh, soon it will be more than just a dream, my friend. Oh, and Claudia, by the way, I know Jake is out of the woods. Don't you worry your pretty little head, he is on my radar as well. We can't leave out the new groom now, can we?"

The doors unlocked. "Here you go. You can all carry on now. Have a good evening!"

Before I could respond, the phone went dead. Josh quickly jumped out of the car, opened Claudia's door, and pulled her from the car. As I stepped out, he made his way around to the driver's side. "Allie, what the hell was that conversation about, anyway? Are you kidding me? A squaw picking berries? What kind of nonsense was that?"

Pulling him into me, I wrapped my arms around his neck. "As strange as that was, I can tell you that things are starting to make sense to me. Listen, let's get some food and get over to the hospital. I'll explain when we're all together."

When we entered the shop, a young man behind the counter greeted us. "Hi, how can I help you this evening?

Stepping up to the counter, I reached out my hand. "I don't think we've met. I'm Allie Callahan."

He grabbed my hand. "So, you're the infamous Allie Callahan!"

I pulled my hand back and shook it out. "Wow, that's one firm handshake you've got there, and yes, that's me!"

Embarrassment showed on his face. "Sorry about that!"

George stepped out of the kitchen. "Well, hello, you guys. I see you've met Samuel. If you told me you were coming by, I would have had something ready for you."

Stepping over, I planted a kiss on his cheek and sighed. "Oh, that's really sweet, George, but this was a last-minute decision. We thought Jake would appreciate something to eat that didn't taste like it was part of something cooked for a couple of hundred people. You know, something besides cafeteria food."

He wrapped his arm around me, pulling me in for a hug. "I get it, sure thing! How about the rest of you? I can put together a tray of assorted small sandwiches, some coleslaw, and chips?"

Stepping over to the jukebox without turning, Josh raised his hand. "You've got my vote. All in favor?"

I looked around the café. "It looks like the ayes have it!"

Within twenty minutes, Sam and George had our food ready and packed to go. I dropped some money on the counter in front of Sam. "Keep the change!"

As I walked out the door, George called out, "But, Allie, this was on the house."

Chapter 33

When we arrived and entered Jake's hospital room, he was watching the news. His dinner was on his tray table and looked untouched. Pulling the cover from his plate, Claudia smirked. "It looks like you have lost your appetite. This meal looks ice cold!"

Waving the remote at the television to turn it off, he rolled his eyes. "You could say that."

When he spotted the takeout bag in my hand, he stretched out his hands and wiggled his fingers. "Please! Tell me that's from George's Café?"

"It most certainly is! We thought you might like a change of menu!"

"That's great. Bring it on over! I have suddenly regained my appetite." Ripping it open, he nodded. "Come on, let's eat. It looks like you brought enough for all of us."

Claudia dug into the bag. "Yes we did, and you don't have to ask me twice!" Pulling out and opening the container of coleslaw, she shoved five plastic forks into it and sat it down on Jake's tray table. Popping open the bag of chips and unwrapping the sandwiches, she grinned. "Okay, dig in!"

We all stood around Jake's tray table and after everyone had a minute to get some food down, Antonio brought up the incident with Allie's car.

"So, I would really like to discuss what happened at George's?"

No one spoke until Jake put down his fork. "What? What the heck happened at George's?"

Leaning against the wall across from Jake's bed, Josh rolled his eyes. "Well, my friend, there was a little episode with Makya outside the café."

Sitting up a little taller, Jake ran his hands through his hair in frustration. "There's no such thing as a little anything with Makya! Are you kidding me right now? What the hell happened?"

Claudia interrupted. "Yeah, Allie, I want to know why you called him Calian, and what was all that nonsense about picking berries and herbs? You told us you would explain when we were all together; and well, we are certainly all together now, right?"

The tension in the room rose as they continued to rifle questions at me. I began pacing around the bed, collecting my thoughts and trying to decide how I might explain what I knew was going to sound downright insane!

"Okay, you're right. I did say that. I am only now beginning to put the pieces together myself. As crazy and convoluted as this is going to sound, I think you should all probably have a seat while I break down this crazy explanation to you."

I turned to Claudia and spoke cautiously. "Remember the night I showed up at your rehearsal dinner? I had no idea I was missing for six months. I thought I had fallen asleep reading a book that Monday afternoon and had a bad dream, but it was a blur. I could only remember parts of it. Well, as the days go by, it seems to be coming back to me little by little. I am beginning to understand that I had somehow mysteriously gone to another time or dimension or something, but I thought that was just too crazy to believe."

I spun around and walked over to the door, feeling like I needed to run from this conversation. Turning back to the group, I continued. "It's kind of a long story, but when I was talking to Makya, I had a flashback. I remembered being with him in my dream or my past, I'm not sure which, but he was an Indian brave named Calian. Wherever I was, it was clear I was his squaw."

Slapping her hands against her knees, Claudia stood. "Allie, are you saying you were his squaw or wife or something in a different life?"

"Yes, that's exactly what I am saying. It seems that we have likely gone around together in a previous life. I don't know, maybe it's all happening now simultaneously but in a different dimension. I haven't quite figured it all out. One thing I know for sure is that this is not the only life we have all been together in. There is more. When I was there, wherever or whenever it was, you were there and so was Josh."

Standing, Josh became wide-eyed, shaking his head and blinking his eyes as if he was trying to reboot what he had just heard. "What?"

Moving to him, I put my hands to his lips. "Please, let me finish. Remember when you asked me to marry you? You said, and I quote, 'This may seem soon, but I feel like I have known you for an eternity. Nothing has ever felt so right!' I think it felt that way because we have always been destined to be together in some way."

Claudia shook her head. "I am so confused. You said in that dimension, Makya or that Calian guy was your husband."

"He was, but as time goes on, I remember more and more about that life and other lives I have lived. I mean, we didn't always look like we do now, but the eyes are always the same. They are the windows to our souls. I can always recognize someone's eyes."

Placing my hand on Josh's cheek, I smiled. "You have always been my calm in the storm, and have always protected me. You were there when I was a young squaw and just a young man yourself. A trapper by trade, you got injured in the woods during the winter months. Some young braves found you dehydrated and sick, so they dragged you back to our village where my great-grandmother, Catori, nursed you back to health. It took you a while to heal and you stayed on with us through the winter. We grew close during that time and by spring we were deeply in love. When Calian went to my father with his suspicions, you were cast out and sent away. You could never return for the risk of being killed. I was promised to Calian, and loving you was not permitted. Without going into everything that is coming back to me, I also lived with you in another time and place. You were a knight. My best guess is in Scotland, but I can't be sure. That is still not clear to me."

Antonio broke in. "But, Allie, what does this have to do with anything going on now with Makya?"

"That's a great question." Turning to the others, I grinned. "Remember in the car how Makya responded when I called him out as Calian? His response was, 'So, you've done it! That's where you were all those months you dropped off the radar.' My guess is that he knows I can move through different times and dimensions. Maybe he has been doing it as well. I think I may have come close to stopping him in some other time and place. More importantly, something in the ancestral box may be the key. If I came close to stopping him during any other lifetime, he must be worried that I am on the verge of discovering how to put a stop to him now, once and for all.

Think about it, why has he traveled all around the country seeking me out to kill me and those around me? All this time we thought he wanted the ancestral box to use for his own gain. I think that it's not as important to get the ancestral box from me for himself, as it is to keep me from stopping his reign of terror once and for all."

Jake slid his feet off the bed to the floor. "All right, I need to get out of here! This guy is way too close and way too powerful! It's going to take all of us to stop him."

Placing my hands on his shoulders, I pushed him back on the bed. "Oh no, you don't! Look, all we have to do for now is keep him from hurting anyone else. It's important to stay just one step ahead of him and keep interrupting his plans. Basically, we need to buy me some time until I figure out what is in that box that he is so afraid of."

Claudia plopped herself into the chair next to Jake's bed. "What do you say we ignore this giant elephant that is looming here with us and change the subject for a while? Let's just drop the temperature and tension in this room and try to have a nice ordinary visit? We have to go back to the apartment soon and get some sleep. It would seem we have a lot more talking to do tomorrow when we get back to the war room at the station."

Sitting on the edge of Jake's bed, I took a deep breath. "I'll second that idea!"

Chapter 34

Two hours later, we were back at the Summit for the night. After Antonio cleared the apartment, we walked through the door and Claudia sighed. "Who would like a glass of wine or a beer?"

Dropping my keys on the entryway table, I replied, "I would love a glass of Pinot if you're pouring."

"One Pinot, coming right up!"

Josh stepped through the door behind me. "I have to go up to the penthouse to see Dakota for a few minutes, but I'll grab myself a beer when I get back."

Stepping in front of him, I chuckled. "A few minutes. Really? You are going to get into a conversation about these new developments and we won't see you for at least an hour."

"No, I promise. I will only be a couple of minutes. I won't say anything to him about what happened today! He can hear about it with everyone tomorrow morning at the station!"

"Sure, he can!"

"No, I promise. I have a surprise for you. I'll be back in less than ten minutes!"

"Okay, if you say so! Can you do me a favor and ask Dakota to bring the ancestral box to the station tomorrow?"

"Sure thing. See you in a few!" He shook his head and gave me that Cheshire cat smile. "I promise, I will!"

Claudia handed me a glass of wine as I entered the great room. "Here you go, girl. I have to warn you, I am not waiting up for Josh. I am finishing this wine and then I'm off to bed."

"No worries. I don't blame you one bit. In fact, I'm not going to wait too long myself. I'm exhausted."

It wasn't even ten minutes later when we heard the apartment door open and close. When I heard him drop his keys in the dish on the table in the foyer, I smiled. "Well, if he isn't a man of his word this evening!"

We couldn't hear any exchange between Josh and Antonio, only a strange clicking sound coming from the foyer as I called out. "Hey, Josh, we're in here. Grab a beer and join us." He didn't answer, as the clicking noise accelerated.

Claudia and I exchanged cautious looks as she reached under the couch cushion, pulled out a pistol, clicked off the safety mechanism, stood, and aimed it at the great room entrance.

Josh walked through the door. Shocked, he threw up his hands. "Hey, wait, it's me! Well, me and my friend here."

As she clicked the safety back on, Claudia scolded him and fell back into the couch. "Why didn't you answer when we called out? I could have shot you."

Turning to her, I reacted. "What the hell, Claudia? Do you and Jake have guns planted all over this house?"

Josh just stood there. "Okay, let's all calm down. It was my fault. You're right, I should have called out, but I couldn't wait to show you, my surprise." Looking down, he boasted, "This is Brick."

Sitting at Josh's feet to his left was a beautiful black and rust Doberman. He had the shiniest coat I had ever seen. The light glistened off him like a mirror.

"Where did he come from?"

"I've had him for a while now. I got him when I was in protective custody. He belonged to a guy named Casey, who was in the reserves and couldn't keep him because he got deployed. He is very well trained and extremely intelligent. Let me show you."

He called out his name. "Brick." The dog immediately stepped around and stood squarely in front of Josh, never taking his eyes off of him. "Brick sit. "The dog sat squarely in front of him, continuing to stare straight into Josh's eyes. When he took a step back, the dog didn't move a muscle. "Now watch, he is so attentive you don't even need your voice." Josh put his hand out in front of him, making a lowering motion. The dog lay down, again never losing eye contact.

Claudia and I just sat there in awe of this beautiful animal.

Josh raised his hand, and the dog returned to a sitting position. Looking over to me, Josh smirked. "Try to call him."

"What?"

"Just try to call him."

"Okay." Leaning forward on the couch, I called out, "Brick!" The dog stood like a stone and never took his eyes off Josh. "Brick, come!" Still nothing.

"Now watch this." Josh gave him one last command. "Brick, out." He kneeled and praised him. "Good boy, Brick, good boy." The dog didn't move but seemed to relax.

"Try calling him now."

I kneeled on the floor and tried again. "Brick, come." The dog immediately turned and came running over to greet me with his little stub of a tail wagging and lots of kisses. "That's amazing! I mean, he is incredible."

Stepping over to me on the couch, he bent down and kissed me on the forehead.

"He is my engagement gift to you. He will keep you safe and give me peace of mind when I can't be around to protect you. Now, I think I'll have that beer."

When Josh returned from the kitchen, Brick was curled up at my feet. "Well, he didn't waste any time making himself at home, now did he?"

I sighed and reached down to pat Brick. "Josh, he is just beautiful. I'm happy to give him a home!"

Winking at me, Claudia smirked. "Hey, girl, I think I feel a pet store shopping experience coming on. How about you?"

"Yes, that's a great idea. Hey, let's go to that new pet store at the mall. I think a big cushy, comfy bed is in order. Oh yes, and a couple of bowls, the kind that comes with a stand for tall dogs, and of course a new collar."

Josh headed back to the foyer. "Wait, you two, before you get all crazy and go shopping." He returned with a large dog bed filled with all sorts of dog supplies and toys.

Turning to Claudia, I shrugged. "Do you think Brick is spoiled enough?"

"Heck no, we need to do some shopping of our own for him."

Josh just stood there, nodding his head in surrender. "I should have known I wouldn't win that battle. I know one thing for certain, we have to be at the station early tomorrow so we should turn in soon."

Chapter 35

The following morning, at seven-fifty, Josh, Claudia, and I arrived at the station and made our way to the war room to find Payne and the entire team sitting at the conference table. The room was abuzz as we entered and Payne greeted us. "Well, who is this fine canine specimen with you this morning?"

A little concerned, I winced. "This is my engagement gift from Josh. I hope it's okay that we brought him today."

"Yes, yes, of course. Come right in. To be truthful, Josh called ahead this morning and gave us a heads-up. I actually like the idea that you have him."

George stood from the table and moved over to us. "So, this is the infamous Brick! Will he mind if I pet him?"

"Not at all. He is the friendliest dog I think I have ever met."

Josh moved closer to Brick. "He is extremely intelligent and has a great temperament, but when he is given a command, he can be very attentive and protective. I wouldn't want to be the one who tries to corner him and Allie."

George backed up. "Well, maybe I'll just admire him from the distance!"

Trying to assure him, I shook my head. "No, George, it's fine. He is a big pushover, but at the same time, as Josh said, he is extremely well trained and intelligent. Come on, just give it a try."

George bent down and reached out. Brick immediately started wagging his tail, as if to invite George to pet him. "There you go. That's right, boy, you and I are going to be the best of friends now, aren't we?"

Payne moved to a table at the back of the room and invited us to an array of drinks, coffee, and breakfast foods. "Come on, you guys, grab something to eat and join us at the conference table. It's going to be a long day and you're going to need all the energy you can possibly get. In fact, it's going to be a long week! Get prepared. I plan to bring in all of our meals to this room until we solve this case once and for all. The only thing we will be leaving this space for is to use the restrooms or to retire for the night. I just received a call from the feds. Their team just arrived and are making their way up from the parking garage."

I turned to Dakota. "Did you bring the box?"

Reaching under the conference table, he lifted it, walked over, and placed it down in front of me.

Payne stood as a team from the FBI walked through the conference room door and paused. "Please come in. We are so glad to have you all here." As they entered the room with three dollies piled high with file folder boxes, Payne continued. "Well, I can see we are going to have our work cut out for us this morning, just trying to get organized. Let's get the introductions out of the way and get right to work."

Going around the table, each of the members of our team introduced themselves and explained how they came to be involved with this team. Detective Hayln from Colorado went first, followed by Brian from forensics, George, Josh, Dakota, Dilson Hill, and me.

The four members from the FBI were Agents Tracy Davis, Lance Taylor, Noah Baker, and Adam Rivera. Once we had that out of the way, we tackled and organized the new boxes of evidence. By noon, we were ready to dig in and get to work. Once lunch arrived, we grabbed a bite to eat and sat down to brainstorm.

Payne began the discussion. "I would like to start with the latest developments in this case and work our way back, comparing our collected files with those from the FBI."

Everyone agreed, and as they began with Alex's murder, she popped in next to me. The minute she appeared, Brick looked in her direction and started whining, as if his heart would break. I reached down and patted him on the head. "It's okay, boy, it's fine!" Looking up at Alex, I nodded toward the door. As I got up, Payne spoke.

"Allie, where are you going? We're just getting started."

I rolled my eyes. "Can't help it, Payne, nature calls!"

He waved a hand at me. "Alrighty then, TMI!"

Brick followed me out the door, and as I got in the hall, I turned to find Alex on my heels. She couldn't contain herself.

"He can see me! Your dog can see me!"

"His name is Brick, and yes, it would seem so."

Brick released a deep, guttural growl.

Grabbing his collar, I kneeled next to him. "What is it, Brick? What's the matter?"

I looked up just in time to see a man standing at the end of the hall, dressed in a three-piece, pinstriped suit, carrying an old leather satchel, and wearing a white fedora on his head. It was one of the strangest sights I had ever seen. Before I could make my way to where he was, he had run around the corner and disappeared. Brick never left my side, but was prancing in place and sniffing at the floor as if he wanted permission to pursue him.

Alex appeared directly in front of me. "Don't let him go. Don't ever get separated from this dog. He will protect you." Then she vanished.

As I made my way back to the war room, I was trying to decide if I should let everyone know what just happened. Really, what would I say? *Oh, by the way, Alex, who just happens to be dead, was here to talk to me. And oh yes, together we chased someone down the hallway? And by the way, that effort was futile, because no one was there when we made our way to the end of the hall?* First, we hadn't even explained my so-called gifts to the FBI agents. Suddenly, I realized it would be much easier if we did that now and got it out of the way. It would make these seemingly unexpected things that happened to me a little easier to explain.

Entering the war room, I approached Payne.

He took one look at me. "What?"

I stepped closer and spoke in a hushed tone. "I thought it might be a good idea to speak with the new members of the team and fill them in on my so-called abilities. It is a big part of what is going on here and, well, I think they need to know."

"You're right, Allie. I just want to make sure you are ready to deal with that fallout."

"Payne, the more time they spend with me as part of this team, the harder it will be to ignore. Things are moving so quickly now. I never know what I may have to explain from one minute to the next."

"You're right. Would you like to address the group or would you like me to?"

"Why don't I start and you can join in when you have something to add."

Payne stepped up to the end of the conference table. "Excuse me, could I have everyone's attention? It's important that Allie and I speak with you for a few minutes. There is some important information we need to share with the new members if you are going to be working closely with Allie."

As the room became silent, Josh stood. "Allie, are you sure you want to do this?"

"Yes, Josh, it's fine."

Stepping closer to the table, I ran my hand over the ancestral box. "Bear with me, everyone, this is not easy for me to say. In fact, this is the first time I have ever tried to talk about this with anyone that I don't know, or have come to trust in some way. Let's see, I guess I will start with this box in front of me. This is not evidence for this case. Well, not exactly! This artifact has been passed down in my tribe from generation to generation. It's known as the ancestral box and the group of investigators on this team from Stanford have discovered that Makya will go to any lengths to obtain it." I looked to Payne. "I'm not sure if that was the right place to start in this story."

Payne faced me. "May I?"

"Sure, please help me out here!"

Payne took a breath to collect his thoughts. "I met Allie when she was attacked by our suspect and nearly killed. Since then, we, including everyone on our entire team, have had to accept and come to terms with the fact that Allie has many gifts. She has the ability to do several things most would never dream of. Those gifts have been unfolding to her since her attack. Makya has been searching for Allie for years and the evidence of that is what you see strewn all around this room. He also has many gifts, but has been aware of them and has been using them for years. Makya has a lust for power and we suspect he is fearful of Allie, as she might be the only one who can put a stop to him."

Turning back to me, he smiled. "That is a really short summation of what we are dealing with here, but the bottom line is he wants this box. We now believe there is something in it that Allie can use to stop him and he will do anything to get his hands on it. I'm sure those of you who are here from the FBI are wondering what I mean by gifts or abilities, so let's just take a couple of minutes to discuss that. I'm sure you have questions."

Payne stepped closer to the table and addressed the agents individually. "Agent Davis, why don't you start. Do you have any questions?"

"I do. We have worked with others in the field that have psychic abilities. Some were able to help us locate victims, while others helped us locate the perpetrators of crimes. Is that what you mean by abilities?"

Looking at Josh for moral support, he smiled and gave me a nod of encouragement. I took a deep breath. "Not exactly. I mean, I have helped locate victims, but in a different way. The easiest way to explain it is that I somehow have the ability to project myself to other locations and observe things there. Up to now, it has been involuntarily and I have yet to figure out how to control it or do it of my own free will. So far, I have just found myself in the locations where someone else needs me."

Agent Taylor interjected. "That's quite remarkable. I have never heard anything explained in that way. Do you have any other abilities?"

Payne drew my attention, placing a small stack of papers on the center of the conference table. "Allie?"

I looked at Claudia, and smiling, she waved her hand in my direction. "Do it!"

Turning to the stack, I raised my hand and sent the papers swirling in the air. Then, motioning to the center of the table, I returned the papers to their original location.

Claudia gasped. "Hey, you're getting good at that. You have a lot more control now."

Agent Baker sat back in his chair. "Holy shit! How the—"

"Heck did you do that?" Agent Rivera interrupted him, finishing his sentence.

Payne spoke up. "And that's the million-dollar question, ladies and gentlemen. Even Allie is still figuring out the extent of her gifts and how she might control them. Now you can see why she is such a threat to Makya."

Agent Rivera stood and moved over to the whiteboards. "So, if I am to understand you correctly, Allie, it was the attack on you that literally dragged you into this investigation. Is that when you started working with the Stanford Police Department?"

"No, not exactly. That was months before I started consulting with them, but in truth, you could say it was Makya who dragged me into this investigation when he started going after those I cared about most. Since I started working directly with this group, I have had many experiences. These gifts seem to emerge as I need them. For instance, against my good sense, I met and had a physical confrontation with Makya in a theater late one night. Although neither of us made physical contact, we were able to manipulate the elements enough to throw each other around the stage without laying a hand on each other."

Agent Rivera spun to look at me. "Why hasn't someone in the government been notified about all of this?"

Payne spoke out firmly. "Because I promised Allie we would keep this on the down-low. She only agreed to help us if we kept all of this information on a need-to-know basis. She doesn't want it made public and, quite frankly, I don't blame her."

Noah raised his hand. "So, are there more gifts we should know about?"

I picked up the box and moved to the front of the room. "Look, I am only beginning to understand the extent of my gifts. For one thing, I can see people in other dimensions."

Lance shook his head as if to clear his thoughts. "Like dead people?"

"Well, yes, that too, but more than that. A friend of mine who also happens to be an officer here at the Stanford Police Department was injured. He was in a coma. When I visited him at the hospital, he appeared as an apparition standing next to his hospital bed and was able to communicate with me. On the other hand, Alex has appeared to me several times since her passing and has been able to help with her own investigation. You can see how this is unfolding for me on a need-to-know basis. In short, it would seem that I am discovering these gifts when I am needing them most." Opening the ancestral box, I held up the eagle totem. "Since I was a small child, my grandparents and parents have called me Little Bird. The eagle is my spirit animal. It is said that when an eagle enters your life, it brings with it spiritual growth. Since I received this wooden chest, that has certainly been the case. There are a number of artifacts in this box that, to anyone else, simply look like old trinkets or antiques passed down for prosperity. But for me, they are tools of wisdom to be respected and used properly. They are not to be worshiped or used to do harm. Instead, each object has a story to tell that has been passed down from generation to generation."

Payne interjected. "I think this would be a good time to get to work. As we review the evidence and timeline of events on our investigations, I am sure there will be more questions for Allie. We can explain and address them as they come up."

We continued to work tirelessly through the afternoon. Dinner came, and we worked on into the early evening. We reviewed the entire timeline of the case and at seven o'clock, Payne called for everyone's attention.

"I think this might be a good place to stop for the evening. We'll be better served by getting a good night's sleep and reconvening in the morning, rested and fresh. Let's call it a day and start tomorrow at seven-thirty a.m. sharp."

Chapter 36

When we exited the station, we found Antonio parked outside, waiting for us. As we approached the car, the back door opened, and Jake jumped out.

Claudia flew down the walkway and ran into his arms. "What are you doing here?" Pushing him back, she tossed him a skeptical glance. "Jake Carpenter, did you have permission to leave the hospital?"

"Of course, I did! I got discharged today at one o'clock, called Antonio immediately, and was out of there by one-thirty. I wanted to surprise you."

As he got out of the car, Claudia glared at Antonio. "Is that true? Did the doctor release him willingly, or was it under pressure?"

Clearing his throat, Antonio grinned. "To be truthful, I think it was a little of both. Jake had to promise to lie low for at least a week and agree that when he returned to work, he would remain on desk duty until he had another appointment with Dr. Weisfeldt."

When Josh and I got to the car, I gave Jake a big hug. "Hey, howdy partner. You certainly look a little worse for the wear, but at least you're in one piece and conscious."

Brick stepped between us, sniffing Jake's hand.

"And who is this friendly guy?"

"This is my combination engagement gift and security guard Josh gave me."

As Jake kneeled, Brick licked his face. "Well, it's good to meet you too, boy!"

Josh shook Jake's hand and pulled him in for a hearty man hug. "Boy, this is great. I think we should get home, have something for dessert and celebrate your release! What do you think?"

"Sounds like a plan to me. All in favor?" We all raised our hands. "Okay, as usual, the ayes have it."

Josh stepped to the back of the car. "Antonio, could you pop the hatch?"

"Sure thing."

Placing the ancestral box in the back, he called out, "Brick, come." The dog immediately responded and ran to Josh, sitting at his feet. He gave him a second command. "Brick, kennel."

Again, without hesitation, Brick immediately leaped up and laid down in his crate. Josh rewarded him with lots of praise and pats. "Good boy, Brick, that's a good boy."

Moving to the back of the car, Jake tipped his head with astonishment. "Well, I'm impressed! I don't know where you found that dog, but he's certainly well trained."

As we all got settled into the car, my cell phone rang. Taking it out of my purse, I checked the caller ID. "It's Payne. Jeez, Louise! We haven't even driven away from the curb yet! Let me get this before we leave. Hello, Payne, what's up?"

"I'm sorry, Allie. Do you mind staying a bit longer? We need you down at the morgue. I promise I will drive you home myself, and I won't keep you more than an hour."

"Okay, Payne, one hour only. I need to get some sleep so I can be at the top of my game tomorrow morning when we meet with the feds again."

"Uh ... about that, Allie." I heard the hesitation in Payne's voice.

"What? Are you kidding me? Payne, what's going on?"

I looked across the walkway to see Payne coming out of the station. Motioning to us, he jogged to the car.

I rolled down my window. "Payne, really? Am I off the case with Makya?"

Scrunching his face pleadingly, he rolled his eyes. "Maybe for just a few days. Come on in, and Brian and I will fill you in on what's going on."

Josh smiled. "You got this, Allie. It's just an hour, but take Brick with you."

Once again, Antonio popped the hatch of the car. I got out and moved around to the back, opening the crate to let Brick out. "Okay, Payne, let's do this."

As Payne and I made our way to the morgue, Brick kept the pace, staying glued to my side.

Entering his office, Brian called out from the lab. "I'm in here, Payne. Come on back."

Just before I went to cross the threshold of the morgue, Brick stepped in front of me, pushing his head against my legs as if to stop me from entering the room.

Reaching down, I petted him on the head. "It's okay, Brick. It's okay, boy."

He moved to my side, and we both entered the room. Suddenly, a heaviness washed over my entire body as if the weight of the air pressed down on me like a vice. Taking a step back out of the room, it dissipated. "Holy shit! What the hell is in that room?"

Brian and Payne stood there, baffled by my remark. Looking concerned, Brian moved to the doorway and stood directly in front of me. "What is it? What's got you so spooked?"

"Brian, who or what the hell have you got in there? The minute I stepped through the door, I felt like the whole atmosphere of the room was closing in and crushing me, making it even difficult to breathe."

Payne shot me a look. "Maybe you and I should stay out in Brian's office, and we'll talk about this case through the observation window."

"That's just fine by me!"

As I stepped to the window, Brian lifted the shade and Payne joined me there.

Brian moved to one of the lab tables where a rather odd-shaped covered object was resting. As he pulled back the sheet, he revealed a bizarre object that resembled a strange piece of art. As I studied it, I realized it was more like a mummified body crushed into a rectangular, cubed shape.

Brick jumped up to gaze through the window and began whining.

"What is it, boy?"

He dashed to the morgue entrance and stood impatiently, moving his feet in place and sniffing at the door.

Moving across the morgue, Brian opened the door. "What is it, boy?"

Brick dashed into the room, directly to the far side of the table, tearing at something on the back edge of the cube.

As I called out, "Brian, what is he doing?" Brick suddenly stopped. He had torn something away from the object on the table.

Running back to the office, he sat directly in front of me and, reaching down, I pulled it from his mouth. Brick had torn a good-sized piece of old leather attached to a handle from the object. "Oh, my God. I saw someone in the hallway today carrying an old leather satchel with a handle just like this."

Brian chuckled. "Well, it couldn't have been this person. They've been deceased for quite a while. By the looks of this body, probably years."

Payne rolled his eyes at Brian and me. "That doesn't mean anything, does it, Allie?'

"Uh, no, it doesn't! By the way, Brian, where did this odd-shaped body come from, anyway?"

"It was found in a car recycling facility. No one knows how it got there, and as we speak, there is a forensic team going over the site where it was found.

"It will probably take us a few days to determine the cause of death, if that's even possible. I wanted to give you both a heads-up, but Allie, I think this is one case your expertise could serve and be helpful. Especially if whoever this is, has already found themself in your presence. Well, you know what I mean."

"Yeah, I know exactly what you mean. An interesting fact is that Brick saw him, too. Brick also saw Alex today. I feel a lot safer knowing he can see the things that I do. It's another set of eyes that I can rely on."

Payne glanced at his watch. "Okay, Allie, there isn't much more we can do here tonight, and I promised to give you a ride home." He turned to Brian. "Don't stay too late this evening. I want you and Allie working on this case first thing tomorrow. If we need you in the war room during the day, we can call you in as we need you."

Brian waved at us through the observation window. "Okay, Payne. See you both in the morning."

Chapter 37

When I got back to the Summit and made my way upstairs, I found Antonio settled into the wing-back chair just inside the apartment entrance.

"Hello, Allie. It looks like Payne kept his word and delivered you back to us in record time."

"Yes, he sure did, didn't he?" I hesitated in the doorway and took a step back. "Can I get you anything? A coffee perhaps?"

Reaching down, he picked up an empty mug from the floor. "Oh, yes, please. How about a refill? Claudia gave me a coffee when we first got back and I think another shot of caffeine would be great."

"Okay then, one refill coming up."

Brick and I moved through the foyer and made our way to the kitchen to find Jake, Claudia, and Josh sitting at the island. Josh sprang to his feet, bolted over, and wrapped his arms around me. "I'm so glad to see you."

"Josh, it's only been an hour since you left us at the station."

Jake piped up. "We were taking bets on how long Payne would keep you this evening. Josh has been as nervous as a kitten since we left you at the station."

Josh laughed. "Really? A kitten?"

Sitting Antonio's mug on the counter next to the Keurig, I added, "I would say more like a lion, protecting his cubs. Claudia, Antonio would like a refill. I sure could use a coffee myself. Are those muffins from breakfast this morning? I could smell them as I came through the door."

"No, even better. Claudia just pulled them from the oven five minutes ago."

"Sweet, I will definitely have one of those!"

Claudia filled Antonio's mug with fresh coffee and put a muffin on a plate for him. "I'll be right back. I want to hear what was so important that Payne had you stay for an extra hour this evening."

True to her word, she didn't waste any time and was back in about fifteen seconds to rifle questions at me. "So, Allie, tell us what is going on with Payne. Why did he ask you to stay this evening? Is he taking you off of the Makya case?"

"Slow down, Claudia. Take a breath!"

Walking to the sink, Jake rinsed his mug and plate under the faucet, and placed them in the dishwasher. "I have to admit Allie, we were all puzzled as to why he asked you to stay. What couldn't wait until tomorrow?"

After a bite of my muffin and a sip of coffee, I cleared my throat. "That's the strange part. I still don't know why he insisted on speaking with me tonight and why it couldn't have waited until tomorrow." I placed a napkin under my mug on the table. "He actually kept me to talk about something that was brought to the morgue that is connected to a cold case."

Jake's face twisted with confusion. "Something or someone?"

"Well, both. Something that looked very old and compacted into a rectangular cube. I mean, it looked like an object that was crushed and intertwined with a corpse. It actually was so old that it looked mummified."

Claudia stood and shook her body to rid herself of the image. "Mummified? That's creepy, Allie!"

I gasped with frustration. "Can we skip the work talk for a while and take a break from all the doom and gloom?"

Claudia moved over to place her dish and mug into the dishwasher, curling up in Jake's arms. "I think I need to turn in, because we need to be up and out of here in the morning by seven o'clock." Stretching up, she gave Jake a hug and peck on the cheek. "What do you say, Mr. C?"

Taking a breath and winking, he pursed his lips. "Hmm, that sounds like an offer I can't afford to refuse, Mrs. C!"

Josh stood, and of course, he scooped me up in his arms.

"Josh, I haven't even finished my muffin yet?"

"Hey, I promise I'll make it worth you sacrificing that muffin!"

As Jake and Claudia left the kitchen, she yelled back, "Hey, get a room, you two! I know we are!"

Chapter 38

Josh carried me off to our room and gently placed me down on the bed. "Stay right here. Don't move. I'll be right back!"

It's clear he didn't make it back in time, because I was so exhausted, I don't even remember drifting off to sleep.

A few hours later, a buzzing around my head stirred me. As I lay there, I couldn't help but notice how warm the room was. Trying to go back to sleep, I swatted at the buzzing sound and it subsided. That silence was short-lived, as a minute later it began again.

Dazed, I opened my eyes and sat up to find myself in a strange place. The room was dimly lit by a kerosene lantern that rested on a wash table against the wall. I was shocked to find myself completely naked, next to a man I didn't recognize. His skin was glistening with sweat from the heat and humidity that hung over the room like a wet blanket. We were on an old brass bed and there was a cotton sheet and patchwork quilt crumpled down to the end of the bed. I reached up and relief washed over me when I felt the tree of life still hanging from the chain around my neck. Standing, I carefully removed the sheet and wrapped it around my drenched body. As I took a few steps across the room, the floor creaked. Turning back to the bed, the salty sweat dripped from my forehead, wetting my lips, and dropping to the floor. The man in the bed rolled onto his back but didn't wake.

I was in a large, one-room hunting cabin. There were several trophy heads mounted on the walls: a moose, a bear, and a buck with the largest rack on it I've ever seen. On the opposite side of the room was a large stone fireplace. Above it hung a hand-drawn map and as I slipped closer toward it, I read: *The Ozark Mountains (Est.1921)*.

Oh, my God, I've done it again. I paused to gather my thoughts. *Okay, I must be here for a reason. Think, Allie. What would I need here?*

I turned to scan the room again, and then, there it was, in the corner on the floor. The ancestral box. Making my way across the room, I kneeled beside it. As I ran my hand over the top, my mind was reeling. *What the hell! Where am I and who is that man in the bed? Is he a friend or foe?* I wouldn't know unless I woke him up. *Wait, I was laying naked in the bed with him. He must be Josh. Yes, that's it! It must be Josh in a different time or dimension.*

Then it occurred to me. *Wait, I did make some bad choices in other lives.* It came back to me that at least in one life I was Makya's squaw.

Making my way to a large chair next to the bed, I sat down. I would let whoever was sleeping wake on his own. When he did, I would let him take the lead with any conversations until I could figure this out.

Fifteen minutes later, he rolled over in bed, stretching his arm to where I had been laying. He felt around for a few seconds, and then he sat up in a panic. Seeing me sitting in the chair, his body relaxed a bit, as he let out an audible breath, "You frightened me, honey." He had a heavy midwestern accent. He slid his muscular, naked body across the bed and sat directly in front of me, and as I gazed into his eyes, my body immediately responded and I knew it was my Josh. Ripping off the sheet, I lunged myself into his arms and shoved him back onto the bed.

"Wow, slow down, honey. We have to get ready. I need to get to the well and bring up some fresh water for us to bathe and make some breakfast. Everyone will be here soon and I don't want to get caught with my pants down, and I do mean that metaphorically and literally."

Well, this version of Josh was well-spoken and mannerly, but the real question was, who would be here soon?

An hour later, we had eaten, and we were cleaning up when I heard him splashing the water in the wash sink.

"Hey, honey, could you please grab me the razor from the nightstand?"

Opening the single drawer, I found a shaving mug and a single-edged razor. Resting them on the wash table, I sat at the edge of the bed and waited for him as he finished. After carefully drying his face and removing the washbowl from the table, he casually walked across the room, opened the window, and dumped the water outside on the ground.

"Okay, your turn. He placed the bowl back on the washstand, wiped it dry with his towel, and refilled it with a fresh pitcher of water. "Here you go!"

Moving across the room, he opened the wardrobe and started rifling through things. He took out the most beautiful white summer dress I had ever seen, made of cotton lace with an empire waist adorned with a silk ribbon that tied in a bow and fell down the back of the dress. He carefully spread it out on the bed and gazed back at me with the most loving smile. It made my heart melt. "I bought this especially for you, my love. I wanted to surprise you. Isn't it grand? Now come on, honey, get dressed or we'll be late for our own wedding!"

I must have turned ashen white at the shock of this news. He ran to my side, scooping me up in his arms. "Are you all right, my dear? Do you like the dress?"

Collecting myself, I shot back, "Honey, now put me down. I haven't bathed yet. I am all sweaty and you have already bathed. There will be plenty of time for this later. I was just shocked is all!"

Stepping away, he slid a suitcase out from under the bed and stepped behind the wooden partition in the corner of the room. "I'll get changed back here while you get washed and put on your new dress. I promise I won't look until you tell me."

After washing, I stood in front of the small mirror that hung on the wall behind the wash table to brush and put up my hair. Moving to the bed, I lifted the dress and slid it over my head. It was a perfect fit. Laying next to the dress was a beautiful, birdcage bride's headpiece, with a soft white feather attached on one side. Stepping back to the mirror, I pinned it carefully in place.

Taking a deep breath, I moved to the middle of the room and called out, "I'm ready!"

The blood drained from my head as the young man stepped out from behind the partition dressed in a blue pinstriped suit, wearing a white fedora on his head. At that moment, my knees went out and everything went black.

Chapter 39

"Hey, Allie, wake up. We have to leave for the station in less than an hour!"

Sitting straight up in bed to get my bearings, I shot him a look. "What time is it?"

"It's six-fifteen and I have already taken Brick out for a walk. I let you sleep in as long as I could. You were so tired last night. You passed out before I could even get you to bed. When I laid you down, you were already out like a light."

Getting up, I started rushing around the room to collect my clothes. "Josh, I have to get to the station. I have to see Payne and Brian."

Claudia knocked on the door. "Hey, what's going on in there? What's all the commotion about?"

"Nothing, we'll be out in a few minutes."

"Okay, Al, but your mom called, and she wants the four of us to come up to the penthouse for supper this evening. She said to call her and let her know if that works."

I cracked the door to look out "Look, Claudia, are you and Jake free tonight?"

"Yes. Remember Dr. Weisdfelt grounded Jake? He can't go anywhere for now."

"Well, sure then, but can you call her for me and let her know? Tell her we will be there about seven, if that works."

"Sure thing! I'll call her back now."

In twenty minutes, we were in the car and Antonio was driving us to the station. The minute he stopped the car, I opened the door and my feet hit the ground running.

"Sorry, guys, can't wait. See you all later."

I ran into the station and headed toward Payne's office when Stacy Anderson called out, "Allie, Payne is down in Brian's office."

"Great, thank you."

As I changed direction and headed to the nearest elevator, Stacy shook her head. "Alrighty then! Good morning to you, too."

As the elevator door opened, I looked back. "I'm so sorry, Stacy. I don't mean to be rude, just in a hurry is all!"

I made my way to Brian's office as quickly as my feet would carry me. Payne and Brian were sitting, having a coffee, and nearly fell off their chairs when I burst through the door.

I stopped short and bent down to catch my breath, "Oh, my God, you guys!"

Payne jumped up and slid a chair to me so I could sit. "What's going on, Allie?"

I turned to Brian. "Have you made any progress identifying the object that was brought in yesterday?"

"Why?"

"Because I may have some information that may be helpful. Well, I might! Give me a minute to catch my breath."

Payne poured a coffee and placed it on the table in front of me. "Okay, Allie, let's slow this conversation down a bit. You seem a little unnerved."

I laughed. "Unraveled is more like it. I literally woke up this morning, took a shower, got dressed, and rushed over here."

"Okay then, what's got you so fired up?"

"I did a little traveling last night while I was sleeping. You know, like the unconventional type of traveling I often do! Payne, the guy I saw in the hall yesterday, the same one I think is cramped up in that cube they brought in, is Josh."

Brian shook his head and blinked his eyes. "Josh? Are you losing it, Allie? That can't be Josh. Last time I looked he was very much alive."

"No, not the Josh we all know today, but a Josh from a different time. Maybe a previous life."

Payne stood and peered through the observation window. "Okay then, help me understand how that could be possible."

I stood up and moved over next to Payne. "Well, Brian, I see you were able to pull some of that object apart. See the navy-blue fabric? That's from a pinstriped suit. And that white wool fabric is from a man's fedora hat."

Brian joined us at the window. "She's right, Payne, that's what we determined."

I went to the door of the morgue and hesitated. "I think I'll try this again." Before I could cross the threshold, Josh walked into Brian's office with Brick. "Hey, Allie, I think you forgot someone."

I kneeled as Brick dashed over to me, knocking me down with kisses. "Okay, boy, I'm sorry!"

Josh called out, "Brick, settle."

Brian extended his hand to Josh. "Good morning! Allie had some astounding news this morning, didn't she?"

Stepping between them, with my back to Josh, I shot Brian a look. "I haven't exactly had time to discuss the details with Josh yet. I thought we would wait until we can verify a few things."

Brian began stumbling over his words. "Oh, sure. Okay, well, that's probably a good idea!"

Payne stepped over to Josh, put his arm around his shoulder, and redirected him to the door. "What do you say we go up to the war room and get started with the team upstairs? I'm sure Allie and Brian have a lot to do this morning." As he left the room, he looked back over his shoulder, "See you two later."

Brian reached down to pat Brick. "Allie, why didn't you talk to Josh about this?"

"For heaven's sake! What was I supposed to say? Hey, Josh, you know what? I think I know who is crushed and twisted up in that compacted cube at the morgue. Well, hold on to your hat, because it's you. That's right, it's you from a previous life!" Realizing how ridiculous that sounded, I clenched my teeth. "That does sound kind of crazy, doesn't it?"

Brian gave me a half-smile and rolled his eyes. "Yeah, kind of. I mean, if anyone else but you said it, I would think it was downright lunacy, but coming from you, well—"

"No need to finish that thought. We have to get to work." I marched back over to the entrance of the morgue. "Let's try this again."

Stepping across the threshold, I hesitated. It was fine, nothing happened. I sighed with relief. "Thank goodness."

I took a few more steps. Brick followed me and immediately made his way across the room where he climbed into a plush new bed, picked up a rawhide bone that was resting in it, and settled in.

"Okay, Brian, where did that come from?"

"Don't look at me. It was Payne. He said if Brick was going to be our new station mascot, he needed a few things." Brian walked over to a cabinet and pulled out two bowls. "One of these is for water and the other for food."

"Are you kidding? I didn't bring any food."

"Oh, he thought of that as well." Walking to the refrigerator, he pulled out a long tube of dog food. With a grin, he started reading the ingredients on the label. "Made with ground turkey, spinach, carrots, and rice."

"Alrighty then, Brick. It looks like you have plenty of supplies for the day. Payne has apparently thought of everything."

I stepped over and stood between two of the exam tables. One had several articles on it which included the fabrics that I had recognized. The other table held the rest of the cube that still needed to be disassembled. I took a deep breath. "Well, there is no time like the present."

"Are you sure you are up to this, Allie?"

"Oh yes, let's get to it."

As Brian pulled back the sheet, he added, "They found a metal trunk last night at the scene and they are going to transport it here today. It appears that it could be what held these contents for years. It's like they crammed all the evidence into the box to hide it. Over the years, the contents took on the shape of the box. Last night we looked at this cube using X-ray technology and determined a number of things. It holds a leather satchel that contains guns and ammunition. At some point, it must have been opened or exposed to severe heat. Something had to have dried out the fluids that would have come from the tangled bodies in the box. We still have no idea how long the contents were separated from the box or how everything got to the car recycling facility."

"Wait, Brian, did you say bodies?"

"Yes, it appears that there are two bodies intertwined in this cube shape. We need to carefully disassemble it today and try to figure out what and who this is."

Brian and I spent the morning disassembling the cube. We laid the body parts out on the other two tables as we were able to separate them.

Brian stepped over to one body. "This is clearly the frame of a man. We need to send some samples of the clothing and DNA to the lab for testing." Turning to the other exam table, he shook his head. "This is the body of either a small framed woman or a young girl. It's hard to say." He hesitated. "Wait, there is something here." Taking a pair of tweezers, he gently teased it away from the hair of the corpse. "This looks to be some sort of netting that is draped across her hair. He placed the material in a large petri dish and set it on the table next to the corpse.

Stunned and taking a few steps back, I stopped to gain my composure. "Brian, that was a hat. You know, one of those birdcage-style hats, or headpieces from the twenties."

"You mean, like in the nineteen-twenties? Like the roaring twenties?"

"That's exactly what I mean. These two must have been murdered on their wedding day, back in the nineteen-twenties. It wasn't just Josh I saw last night when I traveled to the past. It was some version of me as well."

"How can you be sure it was you?"

"Because last night I relived it. I was awakened by the heat and a mosquito buzzing around my head. When I sat up, I realized I was in some sort of hunting lodge."

"Do you have any idea where you were?"

"I might. There was a hand-drawn map over the fireplace that was dated nineteen twenty-one. It was a map of the Ozarks in Missouri."

"Are you sure? In Missouri?"

"I'm positive. To make a long story short, I came to realize that the man with me in the cabin was Josh. To surprise me, he bought me a beautiful cotton dress and that hat for our wedding day. Apparently, we were expecting guests, and we were getting cleaned up when he stepped out in that blue pinstriped suit and fedora. I think I was so shocked, that I passed out. The next thing I knew, I was waking up in the apartment at the Summit, back in my own time."

"Shit, Allie! Is there anything else I should know?"

"Yes, Brian! Alex, Brick, and I saw a man in the hallway at the station yesterday. It must have been Josh from the nineteen-twenties. He was wearing that suit and hat when I saw him."

"Well, Allie, let's keep working and get the rest of this object taken apart. I would like to have it done by the end of the day."

By four-thirty, we separated the last of the objects from the center of the cube. It was what was left of the brown leather satchel and its contents. As Brian pulled out the first gun, I was stunned.

"Isn't that some sort of automatic weapon?"

"Yes, it is. The type that the mob used back in the twenties. Did you know that the mob actually used automatic and semi-automatic weapons back then, out-gunning the police who carried .38-caliber revolvers and sometimes 12-gauge pump-action shotguns?"

"Are you kidding? That's crazy!"

"It sure was."

"Wait, Brian. Josh was carrying this bag. I can't believe he was ever part of the mob! It's just not like him!"

The office phone rang and as Brian went to get it, he shot back, "Well, Allie, I guess it's up to us to figure that out."

While I was waiting for Brian, I stepped over to the lab table, looked down, and touched the satchel.

"Hey, Allie!" Looking up, Alex was standing right in front of me.

"Hey, Alex. What's up?"

"Trust your instincts! Josh could never be on the wrong side of the law. I have to go soon. There is nothing more for me to do here. You can figure the rest of this out for yourself."

"Alex, what are you talking about?"

"You've got this, Allie! You and only you can get this done. You have to confront Makya on your own. Only you can stop him. The key is in that satchel and the tool you need from the ancestral box hangs around your neck."

Alex was fading from my view. "But, I don't get it?"

As she continued to fade, her voice became distant. "Allie, you must stop him, one on one. Find him in the twenties. His name was Leroy then. Remember, the key to all this is in the satchel!" That was the last thing I heard her say as she faded away.

Brick stood at my feet with his leash in his mouth, whining. Looking down at him, I smiled. "Well, aren't you a good boy?" Hooking the leash to his collar, I stepped out of the morgue into Brian's office just in time to see Payne coming through the office door.

"Hey, guys, how's it going?"

Brian placed his hand over the mouthpiece of the phone. "They're on the way over with the metal trunk and should be here in about five minutes."

Payne turned to me. "Where are you headed?"

"Brick needs to go out and stretch his legs a bit. I'm going to walk him and then I'll be back."

"Not alone, you're not. I'll go with you. After they deliver the trunk, I think the two of you should call it a day. We're done upstairs and I think Antonio is back to take you all to the Summit."

As I moved to the office door, Josh walked in. "What do you say, are you two are ready to call it a day."

I handed him Brick's leash. "Almost. We are just waiting for something and then we can go. Could you take Brick out to let him walk for a few minutes? I'll be there in ten, I promise."

"Sure thing."

Payne followed Josh. "Hey, wait. I'll walk out with you."

As Brian finished his phone call, the bell at the back door of the morgue rang.

"Come on, Allie. That must be the trunk."

As Brian went to sign for the delivery, I returned to the lab table to take one last look at the satchel. When I moved it across the table, a key slid out from a tear in the bottom of the bag. It suddenly occurred to me. Alex was literally talking about a key. Picking it up, I slid it into my pants pocket."

Brian turned. "Well, Allie, I think we should take Payne's advice, and call it a day. What do you say?"

"I couldn't agree more! As Claudia would say, 'Let's blow this Hoodsie Stand!'"

"Come on, Allie, I'll walk you out."

Chapter 40

Promptly, at six forty-five, we arrived at my mother's penthouse. As we stepped off the elevator, soft jazz was coming from the speaker system. I called out, "Mom, we're here."

Coming from the kitchen, she greeted us at the threshold. Josh pulled a bottle of wine out from behind his back and Jake presented her with flowers. Grinning from ear to ear, she turned to Claudia and me. "You certainly have a couple of extremely thoughtful gentlemen here. Better keep an eye on them, girls. Don't let them get away!"

Josh reached out and kissed her on the cheek. "I must confess, Jake and I are only delivering them. Claudia and Allie actually picked them up."

Turning to lead us into the dining room, she looked back over her shoulder. "Wow, and they are honest as well! Come on in and have a seat. Your timing is just perfect. We have the salads already at the table and we just took the prime rib out of the oven to let it rest before we carve it."

Guile peaked out from the kitchen. "Christina, honey, could you give me a hand?"

I turned from the table. "Can I help?"

"No, sweetie. Why don't you start with your salads and help yourselves to some bread? We will join you in one second."

They returned right away with the open bottle of wine. Guile held it up. "Anyone?" As we all raised our hands, he chuckled. "Well, I guess that's a yes!"

When we finished our salads, Mom and Guile brought out the main course, which was just amazing. Cooked to perfection, Guile served the prime roast with roasted potatoes and fresh asparagus spears.

As they placed the plates on the table in front of us, Josh's eyes lit up. "Wow, I could get used to this. Christina, does he always cook for you like this?"

"We take turns, but I tell him constantly that he missed his calling. He should have been a chef."

Lifting her glass, Mom became a little more serious in her tone. "Since this is your first dinner in our home as Mr. and Mrs. Carpenter, I would like to propose a toast to you two newlyweds."

I raised my glass.

"To the newlyweds!"

Everyone joined in and in unison, we repeated, "To the newlyweds!"

Claudia stood. "And I would like to propose a toast to the newlyweds of the future, Allie and Josh."

A vision of Josh stepping out from the partition in the three-piece, pinstriped suit came rushing back to me. Raising my glass again, I swirled the wine around in the glass. I became transfixed on it, feeling like I was going into a hypnotic state. For the first time, I was aware of my ability to leave my body, causing me to lose my grip on my glass. It fell from my grasp, shattering the crystal, and splattering its contents across the floor, startling me back to reality.

Josh brushed his hand along my cheek, bringing my attention in his direction. "Allie, honey, are you all right?"

I stumbled up from my seat. "I'm so sorry. Could you all excuse me for a few minutes?"

Trying to regain my composure, I headed into the bathroom. Closing the door, I leaned back against it, hoping for a few minutes of privacy. My mind began flashing with images of everything from Josh's glistening body laying in the bed at the hunting lodge to the image of the two of us crammed into that cube at the morgue. I moved and stood in front of the vanity, gazing in the mirror. Reaching into my pocket, I pulled out the key I got from the satchel, placing it on the sink. Unclasping the chain around my neck, I slid the key on it, next to the tree of life. "Why did I react like that? The mere mention of a wedding set off a whole plethora of feelings and images. I mean, we are engaged, but honestly, Josh and I haven't even discussed it since he got back. What if he doesn't even want to get married with everything that has happened?"

There was a knock at the door. "Al, are you okay?"

It was Claudia. I opened the door. "I'm fine. I'll be right out. Give me another second."

Stepping back to the mirror, I straightened my hair, collected myself, and turned back to her.

"Are you sure you're, okay?"

"I am now. Let's go back and join the others."

Sitting back at the table, I apologized. "Sorry about that."

"It's okay, honey. Hey, what do you say we have some coffee and dessert? I made cheesecake with strawberries!"

Jake stood. "Yum, that's my favorite. Let's all help clear these plates and have that cheesecake."

After we cleared the table, I stepped into the kitchen to find Mom cutting the cheesecake, placing each piece on a serving tray. When I reached over to pick it up, the key around my neck caught her eye.

"Allie, where on earth did you come across that key?"

"I found it in an old bag. Why?"

"Because there is an old picture album in your father's things somewhere. It has an old photograph in it of an old player piano. You know, one of those ragtime pianos. There was a key just like that, hanging around the neck of someone in the picture. The reason it caught my eye was that it was such a beautiful, but odd-looking key. Your dad said it must have gone with the old piano in the photograph, and the man in the picture was likely the person who maintained it."

"Really? How interesting."

I certainly didn't want to open that can of worms. The key would have to be part of a conversation for another time, so I quickly changed the subject.

"So how about the next time we get together for a meal, Claudia and I cook?"

The rest of the evening was so relaxing. There was no talk of weddings, work, or anything stressful. Just plain old small talk.

It was nine-fifteen when we got back down to the apartment. Antonio was sitting by the door with the dog at his feet. When Brick saw us, he looked up, stared at me for a few seconds, and then put his head back down on his front paws.

Antonio smirked. "Looks like someone's put out that you didn't take him to dinner!"

Kneeling, I kissed Brick on the head. "I'm sorry, boy, but you were in good hands."

When I stood and moved into the great room, Brick got up and followed me. Looking down, I laughed. "I knew you couldn't stay mad."

Turning to face Josh, putting my arms around him, I gently planted a kiss on his lips. Sliding my hands down his neck, I grabbed his collar, pulling him toward the bedroom, calling out, "Goodnight, everyone. Josh and I are going to bed. See you all in the morning!"

Brick followed Josh and me into the bedroom, went directly to his big cushy bed, and lay down. I kneeled and hugged his neck. "You are such a good boy, Brick. We are so lucky to have you with us. We're going to give you the forever home you deserve."

Josh climbed into bed and pulled up the covers. "I think maybe I had just one glass of wine too many. I can't seem to keep my eyes open."

"That's okay Josh, I think I will take a quick shower and I'll come right to bed."

By the time I got back and sat down on my side of the bed, Josh was sound asleep. Laying down, I began thinking about that glass of wine at dinner and the sensation I got as I began swirling it in the glass. It was the first time I felt myself slipping from my body. If I hadn't lost my grip and shattered it on the floor, I think I would have slipped away again right there in front of everyone.

I lifted the chain from around my neck and stared at the tree of life and key. *That's it. I think I can willingly and purposely travel back to the hunting lodge.* Focusing on the necklace, I began spinning it in a circle. Dazed, I brought my attention to the memory of the hunting lodge and I was suddenly thrust back to that time, once again waiting for that version of Josh to step out from behind the partition.

This time I was prepared and as he walked out, a single tear slid down my cheek.

Moving across the room, he took my face in his hands and wiped the tear from my cheek with his thumb. He used my name for the first time. "What's the matter, Anna, my dear?"

"Nothing, you just look so handsome, is all."

There was a knock at the door, and a voice called out, "James, we're going to be late! Are you both ready? We need to get to the chapel."

Wow, we were James and Anna. I loved those names. They were so simple, but still elegant. James turned to face me. "Are you ready, honey?"

His smile nearly took my breath away. "I am."

"I have one more gift for you." He pulled a small and elegant pearl covered clutch from behind his back. Opening it, he exposed the contents to me. "Just in case, my dear."

We stepped out of the lodge to a wooden porch and at the bottom of the stairs was an old Model T Ford. James reached out and shook the man's hand. "Well, Jeremy, I guess this is it. Are you ready to stand up for me?"

Nodding in agreement, he turned to face me. "Your ride awaits!"

My heart skipped a beat! The eyes once again gave away the identity of the person in front of me. His name was Jeremy in this life, but I knew him as Dakota.

We got in the car and he drove us about a mile down a dirt road to a small wooden chapel.

James turned to me. "Next time I lay eyes on you, we will become Mr. and Mrs. James Smith."

"Yes, we will!"

Chapter 41

Jeremy and I waited in the car while James went up the stairs and disappeared into the chapel. Five minutes later, he opened my door, helped me out of the car and up the stairs and into the entryway of the chapel. When the piano in the front of the church began playing, Jeremy escorted me from the back of the sanctuary and up the aisle to James, who was standing on the altar, beaming from ear to ear.

There were only a few attendees in the pews.

The ceremony was short but beautifully done. When it was over, the pastor announced, "James, you may now kiss your bride." As James kissed me, I could feel that strong and familiar connection I knew so well.

Interrupting, the pastor chuckled. "Okay, James, come up for some air. It's time to walk your new bride to the hall in the next room for a small celebration with your family."

As we entered the small reception area, several people stood around a piano as it played ragtime music. The tune sounded familiar, but I couldn't quite place it.

As James and I moved across the room, the group moved away, exposing an old player piano. On the floor next to the piano was that brown leather satchel.

When the gentleman on the piano stool spun around to face us, he reached down for something at his neck and a look of panic washed over his face. Staring into his eyes, I saw Makya looking back. I could tell by his expression that he recognized me, not as the bride, but as his nemesis.

Lifting the chain to pull the key and my pendant out from the front of my dress, I called out across the room, "Is this what you're looking for?"

His expression spoke volumes. He knew it was over.

Opening the small pearl clutch, I pulled out a small .38-caliber pistol. With both hands, I firmly gripped it, aimed, and pulled the trigger.

About the Author

From a very early age, CJ Carson was inspired by a great story. What brought her to this juncture in life and inspired her to put pen to paper are the many rich experiences and opportunities of her life's journey.

While working in the medical field, she explored energy work and became a Polarity Therapist and Reiki Therapist.

Exploring acting brought her into the world of theatre both on the stage and behind the scenes.

Painting introduced her to a group of artists that shared her passion for bringing a scene to canvas.

Her love of singing allowed her to travel twice to Europe as a soloist with conductor Sonja Dahlgren Prior, who inspired her to do something, she never dreamed possible.

CJ Carson has always wanted to write. *Murderous Interruptions* is the second installment of her trilogy, Veils of Parallel Times.

Follow CJ Carson on Social Media:
Facebook and Twitter: @cjcarsonauthor

Visit her website:
www.cjcarsonauthor.com

Made in the USA
Monee, IL
02 March 2022